Fireballs e
debris in a

The concussive blast of a nearby explosion knocked Bolan and Yerzim to the ground. In a heartbeat the Executioner was up and running, yanking the Israeli to his feet.

The Mi-24 gunships continued to pound the prison, giant chunks of rubble hurtling into the sky. The entire compound became a blinding white light of massive explosions.

Bolan and his companion sprinted in a zigzag as a line of minigun fire swept over the Land Rovers. Several of the vehicles were turned into roiling balls of fiery scrap.

The Executioner kept pumping his legs, straining to reach cover. As he began to launch himself over the wreckage, he felt one final earth-shattering explosion. He was aware of being airborne, felt the heat of the blast clawing at his heels.

Then Bolan hit the earth and everything went black.

MACK BOLAN ®

The Executioner

DON PENDLETON'S

EXECUTIONER®
HELL ROAD

A GOLD EAGLE BOOK FROM
WORLDWIDE®

TORONTO • NEW YORK • LONDON
AMSTERDAM • PARIS • SYDNEY • HAMBURG
STOCKHOLM • ATHENS • TOKYO • MILAN
MADRID • WARSAW • BUDAPEST • AUCKLAND

First edition January 1996
ISBN 0-373-64205-9

Special thanks and acknowledgment to
Dan Schmidt for his contribution to this work.

HELL ROAD

Printed in U.S.A.

Justice is truth in action.

—Benjamin Disraeli
1804–1881

I've been resolute in the pursuit of justice for those who prey on society. I will not swerve from my chosen path until my skills are no longer needed.

—Mack Bolan

THE
MACK BOLAN®
LEGEND

Nothing less than a war could have fashioned the destiny of the man called Mack Bolan. Bolan earned the Executioner title in the jungle hell of Vietnam.

But this soldier also wore another name—Sergeant Mercy. He was so tagged because of the compassion he showed to wounded comrades-in-arms and Vietnamese civilians.

Mack Bolan's second tour of duty ended prematurely when he was given emergency leave to return home and bury his family, victims of the Mob. Then he declared a one-man war against the Mafia.

He confronted the Families head-on from coast to coast, and soon a hope of victory began to appear. But Bolan had broken society's every rule. That same society started gunning for this elusive warrior—to no avail.

So Bolan was offered amnesty to work within the system against terrorism. This time, as an employee of Uncle Sam, Bolan became Colonel John Phoenix. With a command center at Stony Man Farm in Virginia, he and his new allies—Able Team and Phoenix Force—waged relentless war on a new adversary: the KGB.

But when his one true love, April Rose, died at the hands of the Soviet terror machine, Bolan severed all ties with Establishment authority.

Now, after a lengthy lone-wolf struggle and much soul-searching, the Executioner has agreed to enter an "arm's-length" alliance with his government once more, reserving the right to pursue personal missions in his Everlasting War.

PROLOGUE

Colonel Sam Yoraam of the Israeli Defense Forces was walking toward the prison compound in the Sinai Desert when he stopped suddenly, put his hands on his hips and scoured the burning blue sky, then the vast surrounding wasteland. Yoraam couldn't put his finger on why, but he was worried. Something bad was going to happen; he was sure of it. The colonel wasn't a man who suffered from bad nerves or was prone to superstition.

He was a veteran of the 1967 Six Day War and the famous Entebbe raid, and had organized and led countless commando raids against terrorist strongholds in Lebanon, Jordan and Syria. Yoraam had had a long and much-decorated career in the IDF. He was considered a national hero and he was affectionately known as "the Old Man" among his troops. Indeed, as the commanding officer of a hastily constructed prison compound that held the world's foremost terrorist—who was awaiting extradition to the United States—Colonel Yoraam felt every bit his fifty-four years of age and then some.

He gave the compound a thorough inspection, his hard blue eyes taking in every detail as if he expected his portent of doom to come true any second. Two dozen Galil- or Uzi-toting soldiers patrolled the perimeter of the one-story cinder-block prison with its row of iron-barred windows. Six CH-53 helicopters were grounded near the C-130 that had flown in the thirty-three murdering Arabs who had been cornered and snatched up out of the Gaza Strip by Yoraam's strike company less than two weeks earlier. Olive-drab tents now bivouacked Yoraam's sixty-strong company, which had successfully completed that daring raid and snagged Aziz Kamal and his Iraqi butchers.

Yoraam searched the east end of the compound. Beyond the dozen Land Rovers and the gigantic fuel bin that held twenty-thousand gallons of fuel, there was nothing but vast and empty desert. The Sinai, Yoraam thought, twenty-four thousand square miles of nothingness, seemed the perfect corner of hell to hold the terrorists. It was land easy to monitor, but every time Yoraam spotted the distant shapes of dark-clad bedouin and their camels, he became suspicious. At that moment there was a clan of bedouin to the east, the nomadic caravan now angling toward the compound. Were they just curious? he wondered. Or were they something else? Yoraam watched as soldiers jumped into a Land Rover, fired up the engine and sped off to direct the tribesmen away from the compound.

Out of the corner of his eye, Yoraam caught Eziel Baumstein striding toward him. A scowl began to tighten Yoraam's face. He ran a hand over his balding pate, agitated that he had to deal with Baumstein at all. But the Mossad agent had been given clearance by the IDF to interrogate the terrorists. Still, he didn't like the Mossad man. Yoraam sensed Baumstein had some hidden agenda. Or was he being paranoid?

The colonel waited as Baumstein strode toward him. The agent was short and lean, had piercing dark eyes, a crew cut and no chin. Yoraam wondered why the man never sweated in the blistering heat of the Sinai; Baumstein certainly had all the personality of a block of ice, he decided. Dressed in a tan shirt, tan pants and wearing black combat boots, the man carried two mini-Uzis in shoulder holsters, a dozen clips and a commando dagger in the webbing around his middle. There was something not only unorthodox and unmilitary about Baumstein, but also something untrustworthy, Yoraam thought, something that was... what? Deadly? Predatory?

The agent pulled up in front of Yoraam and gave the colonel a cold eye. He hooked his thumbs inside his mini-Uzis and stood, splay legged.

"I understand the Americans are en route," Baumstein said, talking in a tone that suggested he was used to giving orders instead of receiving them. "I wish to interrogate Kamal again before they arrive."

"The Americans will be here in about fifteen hours. You will have plenty of time to interrogate the prisoner again, Mr. Baumstein. Later."

Baumstein stiffened with anger. "Later may be too late. Once the Americans pick them up, Mossad will lose its last chance to get the information it needs regarding other terrorist activities inside our nation's borders. Colonel, need I remind you that I have been given full and complete authority on this base of yours to do as I see fit to—"

"You have reminded me the entire week you have been here," the colonel interrupted. "If you have not learned any more by now about other possible terrorists inside Israel, then I suggest you return to Tel Aviv, or even better, the West Bank, to learn the truth. You are merely chasing ghosts here."

"What is that supposed to mean?"

"It means that I believe someone has betrayed Israel. Someone with authority helped to infiltrate enough of those terrorists inside the borders of Israel and arm them with enough explosives to be able to murder close to a hundred of our citizens. Someone who was not Arab."

Baumstein hesitated. "Preposterous."

"Is it?"

The Mossad agent gave Yoraam a penetrating stare. "Doesn't it bother you, Colonel, that the Americans are claiming extradition rights to the world's most notorious terrorists over Israel's right to prosecute them?''

Yoraam heaved a breath, biting down his mounting irritation. ''Kamal and his butchers bombed the United Nations and set off a series of explosions in New York City immediately after that, which claimed the lives of not only 113 Americans, but also wiped out an entire Israeli diplomatic envoy in that city. Why are you so determined to keep them on Israeli soil? It is far too dangerous to keep those mad dogs on a leash in Israel when you know full well our nation is surrounded by enemies who would destroy us just to free them.''

Baumstein smiled coldly. ''Of course, Colonel, I understand. You feel some allegiance to the Americans, especially their CIA, which helped you get Kamal in the first place, or so the CIA wants to think. Without Mossad intelligence, though, you and your men would never have caught Kamal and his thugs in Gaza.''

''I believe I know where you are headed with this, Mr. Baumstein. You wish to tell me next that we captured most of them, not all of them.''

''Precisely. Do not forget the Israeli soldier and his family who were murdered last week. Remember what the terrorists scrawled in their blood on the walls of his home? 'Kamal will be freed or he will be crushed. Death to Israel and America.'''

"Well, that is why I am here, Mr. Baumstein, to make sure Kamal is sent to stand trial in America, where he will no longer be Israel's problem."

"It is my whole point entirely, Colonel. The ones who are still free have openly pledged to either break Kamal out or make sure he never leaves the Middle East alive. We still have terrorists inside Israel. Kamal has the information Mossad needs."

"Kamal is going to tell you nothing. If you will excuse me."

As Yoraam walked off, Baumstein called, "I will expect to see the prisoner one last time, Colonel."

Yoraam stopped cold in his tracks. "I will allow you to speak with the man one last time. I will have one of my men present, and you will speak in English, not Arabic."

Baumstein looked offended. "You are overstepping your bounds, Colonel. How dare you imply you do not trust me."

The colonel walked on, ignoring the Mossad man, who was talking about a written report to the IDF about the lack of cooperation he was getting. Baumstein might as well have been talking to the desert. Yoraam felt himself become cold and single-minded.

As the colonel closed on the prison, he felt Kamal's eyes on him before he saw the eyes watching him. He kept walking, but he locked stares with the terrorist. A swarthy, bearded face with a beaked nose and dark eyes watched the colonel from behind the barred window with that irrational centuries-old hate that Yoraam had seen countless times in his life. Kamal was a mass murderer, nothing more than a butcher of innocent men, women and children. The man's very existence in the world was an abomination to all life.

A white-hot rage began to boil in the colonel. He had witnessed Kamal's work firsthand. In his mind, against his will, he saw the bodies of victims, strewed all over streets and marketplaces in Israel, saw some of the children who had survived, whisked away in ambulances but who would have to spend the rest of their lives without an arm or a leg or an eye. For just a moment Yoraam had the fleeting idea to walk into the man's cage, draw his 9 mm Beretta and hand the Iraqi butcher the ultimate sentence. Maybe he would do just that. It seemed unjust to let the Americans have Kamal, to merely put him away for life without parole, when the bastard would have been sentenced to hang in Israel. Surely there was a better way.

1

Robert Gorman suspected he was going to have to make an example of two malcontents in the worst way. The former Special Forces major and ex-CIA paramilitary operative salved his conscience by telling himself that what he was about to do was completely and absolutely necessary. If he didn't follow through now, he could lose control of his men, risk a potential mutiny and jeopardize the entire operation. Not to mention the loss of twenty million dollars. It was time to set some matters to rest. Permanently.

Gorman moved out of his tent, squinting against the blazing sun that burned like a furnace over this remote corner of southern Jordan. He stopped and clenched his jaw. The tension in his belly was so tight with a poison to kill that it felt as if he had a coiled viper down there. Two unhappy bastards, he thought, trying to throw a monkey wrench into things at the eleventh hour. For a long moment, steeling himself for what he must do, Gorman peered at the giant sand-colored tent, just beyond the fuel drums, where his men were bivouacked. He wondered if any of the others felt the same as the two Germans. There was only one way to find out.

Dressed in buff-colored camouflage fatigues, Gorman was a six-foot-four, 220-pound block of chiseled granite. He had one big sinewy hand draped over the butt of a holstered stainless-steel Colt .45, and the other hand rubbed the engraved death's-head on the gold hilt of a Fairbairn-Sykes commando dagger. With the fierce heat, beads of sweat broke out on Gorman's long, lean, broad face, his crew cut and the old knife scar on his cheek making his face appear every bit as ominous as the death's-head on his dagger.

He touched the scar. It was an old wound from Vietnam, but one he'd earned in a bar fight in Saigon with four CIA goons who thought they were a little tougher, deserved a little more respect than some "Special Forces prima donna," as they had so unfortunately, for them, put it. Well, four broken and bloodied goons later, two of them damn near shipped home in body bags, Gorman was heading out the door with a bottle of whiskey and his own Miss Saigon, who had stitched up his face and given him one long night of much-earned loving care. So much for prima donnas.

Gorman turned and looked at his right-hand man. Paul Reuter was ex-Recces, a former member of one of the toughest commando units in the world. The blond, blue-eyed south African weighed two hundred pounds, which was spread over a broad, short-legged,

six-foot-tall body. At first glance it would appear that
Reuter wasn't much, but just because the man liked his
beer, cigars, red meat and women didn't make him any
less tough. One look at the steely determination in
Reuter's eyes, the iron set to his square jaw and Gorman could well imagine this South African commando not having much trouble enduring the forty-
two weeks of murderous training in Zululand that
broke ninety percent of all "wannabe" Recces.

Gorman and Reuter went back years, fighting the
bush wars in Angola and Rhodesia, killing guerrillas,
Russians and Cuban terrorists in the hopes of saving
the lower Africa from communism, tribal warfare and
barbaric dictatorship that had torn apart and decimated so much of the continent. Gorman trusted
Reuter with his life.

"You sure you want to do this?"

Gorman returned Reuter's deadpan expression with
a hint of ice in his eyes. "It's not a question of what I
want to do. Let's get it over with."

The two men crossed the compound, which had
been hastily constructed at dawn. The GAZ-66 transport truck and the seven Russian-made attack helicopters were hidden beneath a sand-colored tarp that
blended in perfectly with the hills just north of the
compound. Those hills, and the surrounding desert,
were watched by six sentries around the clock. Gorman knew if they stayed in the area more than a day
they risked detection by roving Israeli F-16s or U.S.

satellite recon. But D day was only twenty-four hours ahead, and more often than not, getting lucky was simply a matter of good planning.

Rolling inside his troops' tent, Gorman announced, "Listen up. I've got a couple of problems I need to take care of."

Gorman's mercenary army of fifty men was scattered around the sprawling tent cover. The head merc raked a hard eye over the sea of grizzled and determined faces. With a couple of exceptions, they were all tough combat veterans of many wars, both overt and covert. Most of them Gorman knew personally; some he didn't. It was *those* men whose loyalty he had to challenge in order to figure out just where it lay. There were Recces Reuter had brought with him, Gurkhas and legionnaires, three commandos from the British SAS and a half-dozen assassins from the CIA's Special Operations Division that Gorman had signed on from the glory days in the lower Americas and West Africa. All of them were disillusioned but hungry soldiers for hire who knew the deal and would go all the way for one last shot at the big time. The men were tough and reliable.

And then there were the two malcontents, sitting apart from the others, in the far corner of the tent, smoking over a hand of cards.

Fortunately Gorman had with him fifteen hardmen from the old Special Forces unit in Vietnam. The head merc had entrusted his life to five of those soldiers many times over the years. He turned his attention to those men, softening his look. Crocker, Collins, Benson, Judd and Hammersmith had been cleaning their assault rifles but now gave their commander the kind of full and instant attention that told Gorman they knew something was very wrong. They were the strong link in the chain, and what they did or said carried weight with the rest of the group.

Gorman put his hands on his hips and pinned the two troublemakers with a hard stare. "Put the cards down. I want everybody front and center."

He waited while his men put out cigarettes, laid down assault rifles and machine guns and formed a semicircle around him. Gorman had to wait a few more moments for Tiel and Mauser. His gaze never left the two Germans, and it didn't escape the big man that Tiel and Mauser kept their Uzi subguns by their sides.

Gorman had never trusted the Germans. Tiel was a former terrorist with the Red Army Faction, but he'd had the necessary contacts in the Arab world that Gorman had needed and used to put together and nail down the final details for D day. Mauser was a former GSG-9 counterterrorist commando who had jumped the wall to join the Red Army for the most basic of human failings: greed. Both Germans had shifty blue eyes almost always hidden behind slit-eyed gazes. Tiel was lean and had a face like a ferret, while

Mauser was stocky and short with a face like a bull-dog.

With Reuter standing behind him, Gorman addressed his army with casual iciness in his voice. "One thing I cannot and will not tolerate is disloyalty or disharmony. Those two things are the death of any fighting unit. In other words, I won't tolerate a man among my ranks who talks in my shadow out of both sides of his mouth. From the beginning I was straight with each and every one of you men. You knew why you were hired, what you were getting paid and what you could expect. I don't need to tell you that in life there are no guarantees. Meaning, we'll take some casualties. And that, people, is the only guarantee I can give you. If someone goes down, he'll stay down. He won't be coming back. If you are wounded and cannot carry or drag yourself for evacuation, you'll be executed on the spot—and that includes myself. That is also the only other guarantee I can give you."

Tiel and Mauser fidgeted. A sheen of sweat broke out on Mauser's forehead. Gorman felt the tightness in the air, read the anxiety and the fear on several faces in the group. One of the SAS commandos, Peter Miller, glanced at Tiel, who was suddenly staring down at his boots. Miller cracked a mean grin, then watched Gorman.

"Now," Gorman said, "about those problems."

Slowly he turned his head and fixed Tiel and Mauser with hard eyes. The tension among the troops thickened.

Tiel looked up from his boots and found himself the center of either everyone's contempt or fear. Mauser looked to Tiel as if seeking assurance. But Tiel broke his companion's stare, looking as if wished he could disappear.

The mercenaries watched Gorman as he strode over to the Germans. Reuter held his ground. Dead silence reigned as the ex-Special Forces major loomed over the two men, until Reuter flicked his lighter and torched a foot-long Havana cigar.

"I understand you two are unhappy with our arrangement. I understand that you think I don't deserve what I'm getting for putting this operation together. I also understand you two are even telling the others that maybe now they don't even need me to pull off this operation."

Mauser became defiant. He looked at the rest of the group, searching for the traitor. "Bastards."

Miller chuckled, a grim sound. "Go on, mate, you've got the floor. Tell the major just how unhappy you are."

Tiel and Mauser sat like cornered animals, but there was hatred in their eyes for the rest of them as both men knew they were on their own.

"Well?" Gorman prodded. "Is it true? Or have I just been hearing stories because maybe some of the others don't like your attitudes?'' Silence, then Gorman boomed, ''Talk to me!''

Mauser nodded. ''All right, I will tell you,'' he snarled, his accent thick. ''Yes, both myself and Tiel, we do not like the fact you come to us, use our contacts to get what you need. There is twenty million dollars at stake, and you are taking twenty percent for yourself.''

''You agreed to the terms, mister,'' Gorman said. ''Fact is, each man is getting well over a hundred thousand in cash. That's more money than you and your buddy will ever see at one time in your whole miserable lives by building bombs to blow up innocent women and children.''

Tiel cleared his throat. ''*Ja*, we agreed to those terms, but we have been thinking our percentage is only one percent. Not much for all we have done for you. We got you what you want. Do not forget that, without us, what is at the end for you would have been impossible.''

Gorman nodded, appearing amused. ''So, what you're saying is you deserve more?''

''Of course,'' Mauser barked, then folded his arms, his face tight with defiance.

Gorman clenched his jaw. ''You can always feel free to leave.''

Mauser shook his head. ''No. We will see this through. I believe that once our man at the end of this mission discovers how you have given us mere dog scraps for delivery of the merchandise... Well, I do not think he will be pleased over your stinginess."

The change in Gorman's expression was instant and terrifying. A veil of demonic fury dropped over his face, but his voice was tightly controlled as he told the Germans, "Maybe you won't see this through. Maybe I don't even need you anymore."

Some of the defiance withered from Mauser's eyes. Now he was afraid.

Gorman lashed a lightning open-handed slap across Tiel's face and drove the German to the ground.

Now Mauser was terrified. "What are you doing?"

"I just slapped your comrade like a woman," Gorman growled. "Doesn't that piss you off enough to want to kill me with your bare hands?"

Mauser didn't move. Tiel touched the trickle of blood at the corner of his mouth, staring up at Gorman with pure hatred.

Gorman cracked a kick off Mauser's jaw, flipping the German over the chair. As Mauser hammered to the hard-packed earth on his back, grunting in pain, the head merc stepped away, removed and dropped his .45 on the ground.

"There, if that'll make it easier for you," he said. "Tell you what. If you can kill me, you can take my twenty percent and be Reuter's right hands. He's already agreed," Gorman lied, then bellowed, "Come on!"

Tiel seemed to think about it for a moment, then leaped to his feet, sweeping up his Uzi. Gorman clamped his fists over the weapon as the subgun stuttered a 3-round burst, punching holes in the tent ceiling. Some of the mercenaries flinched, obviously fearing a wild sweeping burst, but Gorman ended the struggle in the next heartbeat.

With a head butt he crushed Tiel's nose in a blood-spraying pulp while Mauser lifted his bulk, drawing his knife and charging. As Tiel staggered and dropped the Uzi, Gorman spun him. With the superhuman strength of combined adrenaline and rage, the big American hurled him sideways at Mauser, who couldn't stop his rampage in time. His knife plunged into his countryman's belly.

Mauser vented a berserker howl and swept his blade toward Gorman's throat. The head merc grabbed the knife arm, went under and came up behind his adversary, twisting the German's arm up and back. Mauser roared in pain before Gorman grabbed the man's hand and thrust down. As Mauser screamed at the snap of bone, the big American fisted a handful of the German's hair, wrenching his head back. In one blur of movement, the dagger streaked from Gorman's sheath and sliced open Mauser's throat. The German dropped facedown in a spreading pool of blood.

It had taken less than thirty seconds for Gorman to dispose of Tiel and Mauser with such swift brutality, but the ensuing stunned silence seemed to last for a full minute. Now came the moment of truth as Gorman looked at his troops. Two of the Gurkhas, Sarjir and Maktar, had risen from their seats. They looked appalled, seemed to want to say something but thought better of it. None of the others had moved. In fact, they didn't seem to give a damn about what Gorman had done. Reuter was puffing on his cigar, watching the others, waiting for some reaction.

Gorman wiped his dagger on Mauser's pant leg, then sheathed the blade.

"We were getting tired of their whining anyway, Major," Crocker said. "I think I speak for everyone here, sir."

Gorman holstered his .45. He nodded, searching the faces of his troops. He allowed a tight smile. For the most part he agreed with Crocker. But he still wasn't sure about some of them.

"Kindly dispose of that garbage," Gorman said, moving past his men. "I'll give the final briefing at 0300."

2

Tel Aviv, Israel

It was going to be a massacre, and Mack Bolan, a.k.a. the Executioner, feared there wasn't a thing he could do to stop it from happening.

Swinging his rental car off Ben Gurion Boulevard and onto Ben Yehudah Street, Bolan spotted the two bearded Iraqi terrorists, more than a block away. Farouk and Habib were already on the move, hustling through bumper-to-bumper traffic that was crawling along at a snail's pace. He saw the terrorists had gotten lucky enough to park their white van illegally in front of a string of pubs, restaurants and outdoor cafés, a perfect killing ground for the carnage the pair was about to wreak. It was pre–happy hour, and this part of Tel Aviv was packed with Israelis in search of an evening of wining and dining, the entire street one long moving cluster of unaware human targets. Hordes of young people were everywhere, a sea of happy faces doing the cocktail circuit in crowded sidewalk cafés.

Forced to stop in the stalled line of vehicles, Bolan silently cursed the traffic congestion, grimly aware that he could never reach the terrorists in time to stop them from detonating their deadly payload.

But it seemed to the Executioner that he'd been unlucky since his arrival in Tel Aviv two days earlier. First he hadn't exactly been greeted with open arms by Mossad. The Israeli Intelligence agency didn't want any more involvement or interference by Americans at a time when they were reluctantly handing over the world's most notorious terrorist and most of his murdering army to Uncle Sam. Not to mention their nation was practically under siege by roving bands of Aziz Kamal's butchers, who were proving themselves hell-bent on vengeance at any cost.

But Bolan had been given clearance by the Justice Department to operate on Israeli turf, thanks to Hal Brognola. And the Israelis had once again, with reluctance, pledged to cooperate with "Mike Belasko," an alias the Executioner sometimes used when working with the U.S. Department of Justice. So Bolan had gone terrorist hunting to the fringes of Tel Aviv, skipping his rendezvous with his Mossad escort, Ben Yerzim, once Bolan believed he was onto the scent of the suspected terrorist safehouse on the outskirts of the city.

When the big American had seen Farouk and Habib load their van with three crates, their long, loose-fitting tunics concealing the noticeable bulges of submachine guns, he had tracked them to this oasis of pleasure by the Mediterranean Sea.

Bolan suspected his luck wasn't about to improve. He jerked his vehicle ahead when traffic began to move, then swerved curbside to a hard-braking stop behind a taxi. The warrior was out and running, weaving his way through traffic, his death sights set on the two Iraqis who hit the sidewalk on the other side of the street, stopped, turned and looked back.

The Executioner was three car lengths away from the van, reaching for the .44 Magnum Desert Eagle riding on his hip beneath his tan windbreaker, when he made eye contact with the terrorists. Even from that distance, Bolan saw cold smiles slide over the faces of the terrorists. They had known all along Bolan had been tailing them, and had managed to lose the Executioner in heavy traffic back on Jabotinsky Street.

Bolan saw the triumphant smile on Habib's face vanish as the terrorist pulled a small black box from his pocket. Adrenaline racing, the big American grabbed the first innocent he saw, fully and painfully aware that he would be able to save only one life. Maybe.

The woman screamed in surprise and outrage as Bolan grabbed her by the arm and hauled her away from the white van. With the strength of rage and fear propelling him, Bolan moved fast and furious, shouting what he knew to be a futile warning, scooping the woman into his arms and weaving through the rolling maze of cars. Out of the corner of his eye, he saw the terrorist aim the box at the van.

Bolan vaulted over the trunk of a car, clutching the woman to his chest, as the white van was vaporized by a tremendous ear-shattering fireball. A huge tongue of flame roared over the traffic, hurling vehicles into the air and catapulting countless bodies in all directions. The warrior shielded his charge as twisted sheets of metal whooshed over them. The ground shook with the force of an earthquake, and he felt the scorching heat of the killer explosion on his face as fire shot overhead. Then there was a second and third blast, both of which seemed more powerful than the first as boiling waves of volcanic fire vomited wreckage and mangled bodies into the sky. Vehicles were thrown through the windows of restaurants, or whipped as if they weighed nothing more than a child's toy, through crowded cafés. Through the screams of terror and agony, Bolan made out sirens wailing in the distance. He stared down at the woman whose life he had saved. She was a black-haired beauty with dark eyes and a full, voluptuous body, not much more than twenty years old, Bolan decided. There was now pure shock and horror in her eyes, her body trembling, as she stared up at him.

"Are you all right?" Bolan asked.

"Who... how did you know?"

"Stay down," he told her, seeing then she was badly shaken but otherwise unharmed.

He rose, catching a glimpse of Farouk and Habib as they moved swiftly down the sidewalk.

Bolan took in the carnage and felt the rage rise from deep in his belly. Dozens of cars were engulfed in flames. Bodies and bloody severed limbs were strewed everywhere. Horribly wounded Israelis were rolling on the sidewalk, clutching their faces or shattered limbs, screaming in agony.

The Executioner broke into a run, oily black smoke from crackling bonfires of twisted wreckage nearly blotting out the midafternoon sunlight. He quickly closed the gap to the terrorists as he rounded the corner on Frischmann Street. Farouk and Habib plowed through pedestrians, bowling over people in their rampage to escape. Bolan had the tunnel vision of anger and retribution, seeing nothing but the two murdering terrorists, his hand unleathering the big .44 Magnum Desert Eagle.

The Executioner saw the terrorists dart down an alley. Reaching the alleyway, Bolan exposed his silhouette for a second, caught sight of the terrorists, then threw himself against the corner, crouching behind cover as autofire chattered and stone chips blasted over his head. A moment later, as the firing stopped, he chanced a look around the corner. Farouk and Habib were brandishing mini-Uzis but seemed more concerned with a hasty retreat than holding their ground and fighting. Still, trying to catch one of the terrorists in the leg, Bolan returned fire, the hand cannon thundering but only striking stone as the terrorists burst through a doorway.

Bolan raced after them, pumped on a fresh burst of adrenaline. He wanted them alive, but he didn't think he'd get the chance to interrogate them about other suspected terrorist hideouts in Israel. He needed information about a rumor he'd gotten wind of—the reason he'd come to Israel in the first place.

As Bolan charged into a narrow, gloomily lit corridor, he heard shrill female screams ahead, heard the commotion of breaking glass and saw shadows diving to the floor. A moment later he discovered he was in a fashionable restaurant.

The warrior burst into the dining room and found instant and utter chaos. He made a beeline for the cover of a stone pillar just as the terrorists turned and opened fire. Twin streams of 9 mm slugs whined off the pillar above Bolan's head. Staying low and moving to the other side of the column, the Executioner glimpsed the terrorists backpedaling for the front door. Men and women scurried for cover, throwing tables into the air. A waiter with a full tray of food was run over by Farouk, glasses, carafes and dinner plates flying through the air as the waiter did a somersault over a table of screaming guests. Bolan moved out, determined to end it there if only to prevent the deaths of any more innocents.

Farouk seemed more determined to reach the front door and flee, but Habib did something Bolan was already anticipating. Habib reached down to snatch a woman off the floor to use her as a human shield, but the .44 hand cannon in Bolan's fist roared. The massive hollowpoint tunneled open a gaping hole in the terrorist's chest. An even bigger and bloodier hole blew out the Iraqi's back as he was launched, behind a crimson cloud, through a plate-glass window and dumped on the sidewalk beyond in a shower of glass shards.

Seconds later Bolan was out the door, hitting the sidewalk. He spotted Farouk dashing through the traffic at a full sprint. A crowd had gathered around the Executioner, but no one was moving; faces of pure shock and terror stared at the big man with the .44 Magnum pistol.

Bolan watched as the Iraqi turned back, spotting the warrior before racing down an alley on the other side of the street. The shriek of sirens grew louder with each passing second, but Bolan didn't see anyone that looked like an Israeli soldier as he took off in pursuit of Farouk.

Moments later Bolan was in the alley. As the terrorist turned to fire, he stumbled, then toppled to the alley floor. Bolan closed the gap.

"Drop the weapon!" the warrior growled, slowing his stride, lifting the big pistol.

Farouk leaped to his feet, triggering the mini-Uzi, but Bolan's Desert Eagle was already thundering. The warrior's aim was true but not meant to kill as the .44

hollowpoint sheared off a small piece of Farouk's flesh at the shoulder. The peal of Magnum thunder washed down the narrow alley, drowning out the terrorist's roar of pain. Then Farouk began to fire wildly, the mini-Uzi flaming and stuttering, forcing Bolan to hug the wall as a line of slugs sparked and ricocheted off the ground nearby. Suddenly the terrorist pitched out of sight.

Swift but cautious, Bolan surged ahead, arriving at a doorway in time to see Farouk tumbling down a short flight of stone steps. As the terrorist landed in a heap at the foot of the stairs, the Executioner descended. The man was soaked in blood, his eyes glazed.

The Executioner sighted down the barrel of the .44 and said, "It's over for you."

The heavy pounding of bootsteps sounded behind him. Turning, Bolan spotted the Mossad man he had ditched leading a dozen or so Uzi-wielding soldiers down the stairs.

"Freeze," Yerzim shouted at Bolan.

Farouk sat up, his bloody face twisted with feral rage.

Out of the corner of his eye, Bolan saw the terrorist clawing at his ankle for a hideaway weapon, the mini-Uzi lost somewhere during his fall. Bolan wheeled, the .44 sweeping into target acquisition as Farouk pulled a small-caliber pistol from his ankle holster. Reacting, Bolan fired and drilled the Iraqi through the head.

"Drop the weapon!" Yerzim bellowed as Israeli soldiers cocked the bolts on Uzis and drew down on the big American.

Bolan turned slowly to face Yerzim. A long moment of tension elapsed, fury clouding the Mossad agent's face. The Executioner held the Desert Eagle by his side.

"Just who do you think you are?" Yerzim snarled, stepping forward to snatch the .44 pistol out of Bolan's hand.

The Israeli dug out the Beretta from Bolan's shoulder holster. "You have a lot of explaining to do, Mr. Belasko."

WHEN YERZIM TOLD Bolan that he was very unhappy with him, the big American thought that was the understatement of the century.

They were in Bolan's room at the Gordon's Hostel, and three hours had passed since the bombing on Ben Yehudah Street. The room overlooked the Mediterranean, and long shadows were stretching over the white sandy beach as dusk fell over the city. The soft lapping of waves breaking on the beach was overpowered by the air rasping out of Yerzim's flared nostrils as the Israeli fought to control his anger and frustration.

Bolan sat in a chair by the nightstand, waiting for whatever the Mossad man was going to lay on him. With obvious reluctance, Yerzim had returned Bolan's weapons, which told him he wasn't going to be deported.

The soldier studied Yerzim as the man paced around the Spartanly furnished room like a caged tiger. Yerzim was a slightly built, gray-haired agent in his late forties. He was dressed in a white sport shirt, gray slacks and wing tips, and carried a shoulder-holstered Walther PPK/S. The Israeli seemed to be wondering how to proceed as he smoked his fourth cigarette in twenty minutes and poured himself another drink from the bar. He checked his watch for the third time in ten minutes, obviously impatient about something or waiting for someone, Bolan decided.

On the double bed was the Mossad agent's briefcase, which Bolan knew contained photos, maps and other Intel on suspected terrorists in Israel. He judged Yerzim as a tough and reliable fighting man, an agent who was committed to the job of maintaining the security of his country. But he was on edge, which Bolan decided was very understandable. He found himself liking the guy, and had always been fully intent on cooperating with the Mossad agent. There was a determined set to the Israeli's jaw, the fire of conviction in his blue eyes. He had the look of an honest fighting man who would go all the way to defend what was right and good. The fact that Yerzim had given

Bolan back his guns and had somehow managed to cut off a tongue-lashing before he knew the facts told Bolan the Israeli agent was a fair and reasonable man.

Yerzim, his back turned to Bolan as he stared out to sea, killed his drink. The man seemed to be wrestling with the awful truth of the moment.

"More than forty dead," the Israeli said, then heaved a sigh, setting the empty glass on the bar top with a hard thud. "Dozens more wounded, most of them critically. The murdering bastards. If I could bring them back from the dead, I would surely be more than glad to kill them again." He turned and looked at Bolan with a world-weary expression. Indeed, the Mossad man seemed to have aged ten years in the two days Bolan had known him.

"Why did you desert me, Mr. Belasko? I am responsible for you while you are in my country. Why? And do not tell me it is because you work better on your own. I do not appreciate this, uh, American cowboy game you played on me."

Bolan put some steel into his eyes, but kept his voice level as he told Yerzim, "I didn't desert you—let's get that straight—and I'm not one to play games. The fact is, I work better on my own."

Yerzim gave him a hard look. "Israel is under a state of siege by terrorists. This is the third such attack in the last two weeks by these Iraqi butchers. This is no laughing matter."

"You see me laughing? Look, Yerzim, my mission here is every bit the same and every bit as important as yours."

"That may be so, but I told you to stay put here and wait for me to return."

"You left, saying you had some urgent business to attend to, left me with maps, names, photos of and possible locations of terrorist safehouses. Time was running out. If you had known where Farouk and Habib had been hiding, you would have already taken them down. I didn't come here to sit around on my hands or have my every move shadowed by people I don't know and have never worked with. That isn't to say I don't trust you. But I had to make a move."

Yerzim drew hard on his cigarette, peered at Bolan and blew a thick cloud of smoke toward him. "And you knew exactly where to go to find Farouk and Habib?"

"I got lucky. I had already checked most of those locations in your file, and they were dead leads. I chose one that was closest to the city. When I got there, those two had the van loaded with what I believed was either dynamite or plastic explosives. I could tell they were at least carrying submachine guns beneath their tunics."

"And you said they spotted you and ran. They also managed to elude you."

"Traffic was heavy. Unfortunately they got lucky. I wasn't about to run down Israeli citizens."

"You had my pager number. You could've contacted me. We could have had soldiers on them, had them surrounded and taken down within minutes. Ah, yes, I forgot. Time was running out, according to you."

"What happened is over, and I regret what happened. Believe me, I didn't want to see innocent people die, and I was doing everything I could to keep that from happening. Even if you had gotten to the van, I can tell you with complete certainty they would have gone out in a suicide blast in the name of God. You'd still have dozens of dead and wounded on your hands."

Yerzim looked away from Bolan. The agent's expression softened as he nodded. Obviously Yerzim knew Bolan was right.

"Meaning we lost a battle but not the war."

"Exactly." Bolan paused. "Look, my country is sending a military convoy to pick up Kamal and his murderers and take them back to the States. When that escort will be arriving, I'm not exactly sure. But I needed Farouk and Habib alive. I needed them to tell me who is going to attempt to break Kamal out of your holding compound in the desert. I needed to know where the rest of Kamal's terrorists are hiding and when the attack is going to happen."

Yerzim folded his hands behind his back and smiled grimly. "That, Mr. Belasko, was part of my urgent business. As we speak, your country has en route a

Special Forces team that is due to land on the Sinai just before dawn tomorrow. Not only that, but Mossad believes that if there is an attempt to free Kamal, it won't be done by his fellow Iraqi murderers.''

Bolan tensed. That the escort was on the way was news to him, but he hadn't spoken with Hal Brognola in more than a day. And the rumored impending attack to free Kamal was not going to be done by Kamal's own people? Then who were the other players? More importantly, when was the attack going to happen? There was a lot Bolan had to know, and he had to learn it quickly. With his contacts and connections within and beyond the Justice Department, Brognola would have gotten Bolan that critical information about the Special Forces task force. Bolan needed an update from Brognola.

''Not only that, but Mossad has also learned of something that, if also true, could prove to be the worst-case scenario since the Iraqi madman dropped his Scuds on Israel during the Gulf War.''

Bolan stood. ''I need you to get me transport to the Sinai right away. If there's going to be an attack, it'll happen at any time.''

Yerzim waved a hand at Bolan. ''Please, Mr. Belasko, allow us the dignity and your confidence that we can do our job. We have a national hero, Colonel Sam Yoraam, in charge of a rather sizable force of Israel's finest commandos. They are holding Kamal and his Iraqi murderers until the Americans arrive.''

Bolan nodded. "I've heard of Colonel Yoraam, and I understand he's a good man. But the fact is I haven't learned any more about this rumored attack on the compound. A surprise attack might not free Kamal, but it would surely cost more lives. We've come to a dead end here. I need to be at that compound."

"We have not reached a dead end. This is what I'm trying to tell you. Patience, please. There's more than just the threat of an attack on the compound, Mr. Belasko. Once you leave my country and this Special Forces escort takes Kamal back to the United States, our troubles here in Israel might only just have started." Yerzim checked his watch again.

"Are you going to get me to that compound or not?" Bolan asked.

"It can probably be arranged, if you insist."

"I insist."

"First there's someone I want you to meet."

"Come on, Yerzim, we're wasting time."

Suddenly there was a knock on the door. The Israeli looked at Bolan. "That would be the special agent who is in charge of counterterrorism intelligence. As you might say, Agent Weisskopf outranks me. I suggest you listen to what she is going to tell you. Come in," Yerzim called out.

Bolan turned. The door opened and Bolan froze.

"This is Special Agent Elena Weisskopf, Mr. Belasko," Yerzim said. "Agent Weisskopf, meet Mike Belasko of the U.S. Justice Department."

Bolan was riveted, but not because Agent Elena Weisskopf was a stunning dark-haired woman in her early thirties. No, right away something else began nagging the Executioner about the beautiful Israeli agent in charge of counterterrorism.

Weisskopf closed the door and looked Bolan straight in the eye, holding his gaze with a penetrating stare. Bolan sensed he was being judged and about to receive more rebuke, but the trace of a warm smile flickered over the woman's face. It was a face that Bolan would have sworn he'd seen before. Bolan wondered why she was looking at him with... what? Gratitude?

She was dressed in light tan slacks, windbreaker jacket and soft-soled black shoes, but the nondescript garb didn't detract from her beauty and a presence that could freeze an entire room of men. She was long legged with a full-figured body that would stand out in a crowd. Why did she look so familiar? he wondered. The long dark hair, the dark eyes, the high cheekbones accentuating a sculpted, striking face made her look so familiar to Bolan that he had an uncanny feeling of déjà vu.

"Yes, Mr. Belasko," the woman said. As she took a step toward Bolan, the jacket opened a little, and the Executioner glimpsed a shoulder-holstered pistol. "I, too, feel like we've already met. I wanted to personally thank the man who saved my younger sister's life."

The warm smile danced over Weisskopf's lips again. As much as he hated what had happened earlier on Ben Yehudah Street, Bolan returned her smile and nodded.

AGENT WEISSKOPF DROVE her Peugeot through the streets of Tel Aviv. Bolan sat beside the woman, feeling his impatience mounting as he waited for her to tell him where they were going and why. Night had fallen over the city. Bolan filled the tense silence by surveying the streets and the sidewalks. There was far less traffic and pedestrian congestion now that word of the murderous bomb attack on Ben Yehudah had spread. Bolan was informed by Yerzim that a curfew was in effect. Groups of armed soldiers were now out in force, and roadblocks had been set up on street corners. An eerie quiet had settled over the city.

When they came to a roadblock, a soldier poked his head into the vehicle. Promptly Agent Weisskopf produced identification. She told the soldier, "These men are with me," and they were allowed to go on their way.

When they were moving again, Bolan turned, looked over his shoulder at Yerzim, who peered back at Bolan. The Mossad man seemed content to sit behind Bolan and chain-smoke.

"You want to tell me where we're going?" Bolan asked Yerzim.

The Israeli drew on his cigarette. "Early this afternoon Mossad captured one of Kamal's top henchmen near the Gaza Strip."

Yerzim paused, meeting Agent Weisskopf's gaze in the rearview mirror.

"His name is Yarbin Kaballah," Weisskopf told Bolan. "We believe this man is responsible for the recent bombing attacks in Israel. Interpol has also linked him to two such other car-bomb attacks in Western Europe. Aside from the fact that he's been very busy murdering innocent people, it would appear he was instrumental in setting up an arms deal between Kamal and a former CIA paramilitary operative who could buy what Kamal wanted from a rogue Russian agent. The Russian specialized in dealing weapons on the black market, selling to any and everyone who could produce the money." Weisskopf turned and gave Bolan a somber stare. "Kaballah has hinted that he's not just talking about AK-47s and RPGs."

Bolan detected an ominous note in Weisskopf's voice. "Then what?"

"We're not exactly sure, Mr. Belasko," Weisskopf said. "I was attempting to interrogate Kaballah. He began to tell us a very interesting but very frightening story. One that involves a large, well-trained and well-financed mercenary force that is going to attempt to break Kamal out of prison with, I am very sad and afraid to say, the help of a traitor inside Mossad who has also been aiding and arming the Iraqi terrorists in

Israel. Kaballah hasn't given us names or details—yet. Before he told us any more, he had the gall to demand complete immunity from his crimes, protection by the very people he has helped to attack and kill, and he wants the guarantee of safe passage to an unspecified country of his choosing."

"Can you believe that?" Yerzim asked quietly. "Guaranteed safe passage to a country of his choosing." The Mossad man grunted, shaking his head. "Where he can probably form another terrorist faction and try his luck on us again. He'll probably even ask for a sizable cash donation from Israel so he can get comfortably resituated."

"I take it you told him no," Bolan said.

"I told him I would check with my superiors," Weisskopf replied. "Of course, we have no intention of giving him what he wants. I was about to proceed with another line of interrogation when I received word of the bomb attack. My sister—her name is Suzanne—goes to the Tel Aviv University. I know she frequents the pubs and the cafés in the afternoon to meet her friends. I know this because our parents, both of them older Israelis who cling to the stricter and more fundamental beliefs our religion, disapprove of her gallivanting around the city in search of a good time. I immediately went to find her." She looked at Bolan. "She described the man who saved her life. Perfectly, I might add."

She paused. "Yes, I am painfully aware that many Israelis were killed and wounded," she said, as if reading Bolan's thoughts, "But I am very grateful to you, Mr. Belasko, for saving my sister's life. I don't quite believe that you are an agent of the Justice Department. I sense you are something far more, but what, I am not certain. Perhaps it really doesn't matter. We're all working on the same side for the same goal.

"I will pledge you full and complete cooperation on the part of Mossad from here on. If you wish to go to the Sinai, I can arrange that. But first I think it would be beneficial to both of us if I interrogated this Kaballah one last time."

"What you've got is a scared man willing to turn snitch," Bolan said. "A snitch will say anything to save himself."

"I don't think so," Weisskopf replied. "We've checked his background. We believe he's well connected to various terrorist factions in the Middle East and Europe and has access to the money in certain known terrorist countries, such as Iraq and Syria, who finance these butchers. We believe he can provide the information we need to track down the other murderers inside Israel. Especially when we find out who is helping to get these terrorists inside Israel and who is planning to break Kamal out."

"You hope," Bolan said. "After you tell Kaballah you're not going to deal with him on his terms, what makes you think he's going to talk?"

As they rode under a streetlight, Bolan caught something dangerous flash through the woman's eyes.

"Mr. Belasko," Weisskopf said, "Mossad has been sanctioned to do whatever it takes to end the attacks on Israel. Believe me when I tell you I will get him to talk."

"They've invaded our borders," Yerzim added, "like cockroaches. What is it one does when one sees a cockroach in his home? He steps on it and crushes it."

Weisskopf smiled grimly, and Bolan nodded. Yeah, he understood, all right. He wasn't about to come right out and say it, but his purpose and his mission were the same as Mossad's. Flush out the cockroaches and crush them before they invaded American soil again.

3

As Bolan climbed the steps to the second floor of the apartment building beside Weisskopf, the woman said, "I already know how this is going to go. I fear it will go badly. For Kaballah, that is."

Trailing the pair up the stairs, wood creaking under his weight Yerzim shattered the tense quiet with his three-pack-a-day cough, then added, "What Agent Weisskopf is saying, Mr. Belasko, is to let her do the interrogating. Believe me, she'll get us the information we need. One way or another."

Bolan gave both Mossad agents a steady look, then studied the grimly determined set to Weisskopf's face a moment longer. A savage glint shone in the woman's eyes, and he sensed a tightly controlled fury about her, firmly believing she would get the information they needed. He had a feeling this was going to be an interesting, and perhaps brutal, encounter. Bolan had no intention of interfering. Weisskopf was owed her pound of flesh. With more than forty Israelis dead and countless more seriously wounded on Ben Yehudah, Bolan knew the agent was going to play hardball.

As they topped the steps, Bolan saw the two Galil-toting Israeli soldiers at the end of the hallway. Those soldiers looked every bit as grim as the apartment complex, he decided, which had all the look and feel of a mausoleum. From the outside the building was dark, had appeared deserted to the Executioner except for the soldiers on the front stoop. Since they were holding Kamal's right-hand man, Bolan suspected the building was either a Mossad safehouse or had been cleared of all tenants for security purposes.

Bolan watched as the soldiers, looking more like apparitions than living beings in the shadowy fringes of the glow of a naked light bulb, nodded at Agent Weisskopf. One of the soldiers opened the door to the last room at the end of the hallway.

"Do not come inside, no matter what," she told the soldiers, both of whom nodded.

Moments later Bolan followed the woman through the doorway. Inside the room another soldier with a Galil assault rifle nodded at Weisskopf, gave Bolan a quick look, then left the room, closing the door behind him.

It was a drab and dingy room, with nothing but a coffee table, divan, three chairs and a small barren kitchen off to one side. The stench of cigarette smoke assaulted the big American's senses. He spotted the ashtray, heaped with butts, on the coffee table in front of Yarbin Kaballah.

Right away Bolan sized the Iraqi as scared but belligerent. Sitting on the divan, the man looked at Weisskopf with contempt and hatred. He stood, placing his hands on his hips. The Iraqi terrorist was a big man, thick through the middle, with broad shoulders, short, curly black hair and stubble on his face. Bolan saw the same irrational hatred in Kaballah's narrowed gaze he had seen countless times in the eyes of fanatics. The man could prove very dangerous, Bolan knew, but on his own terms.

"Well?" Kaballah growled.

Bolan moved to the corner of the room, waiting, watching. He fixed a steely gaze on Kaballah, who was looking the three of them over with unwavering hate. Yerzim took a chair beside the divan and fired up a cigarette.

"Well what?" Weisskopf asked, holding the Iraqi's stare.

"You have left me here alone for hours. I've had nothing to eat or drink, I am even made to feel as if I should beg your soldiers for a cigarette. You tell me nothing and leave suddenly. Now you return with these two, who look as if they wish to rip me to pieces and feed me to wild dogs. Is this how you treat a man who has agreed to cooperate with you?"

Weisskopf stripped off her jacket and threw it on the divan. Anxiety flickered through Kaballah's gaze as he looked at the woman's holstered Walther.

The Iraqi jerked a nod at Bolan. "Is this your superior who will give me what it was I asked for?"

Slowly Weisskopf walked to the coffee table to stand almost nose to nose with the Iraqi terrorist. Bolan observed her as she pinned the Iraqi with a cold look, sensing there was something deadly about the woman.

"The gentleman behind me is neither my superior, nor am I prepared to give you what you want," she stated.

"What are you telling me? We had a deal."

"The only thing I am prepared to grant you," Weisskopf said, "is life over certain death."

"You stupid Jew bitch," Kaballah snarled, "we had a deal."

Suddenly Weisskopf lashed a backhand across the Iraqi's face, rifling the air with a loud crack of flesh on flesh. He hit the divan like a felled tree. Touching the the trickle of blood at the corner of his mouth, Kaballah looked at Weisskopf, stunned for a moment, then bellowed in rage and leaped to his feet.

Weisskopf moved to one side of the coffee table, holding her ground, leaving herself exposed, her hands by her side as Kaballah charged her. The Iraqi threw a wild looping right at the woman's head, a blow meant to shatter her face. Weisskopf ducked the roundhouse with catlike grace, then pounded a fist into the Iraqi's kidney. With the wind belching from Kaballah's mouth, she clipped a kick into the back of the Iraqi's leg, dropping him on his back.

"Now, do you talk or would you like me to continue?" Weisskopf rasped down to Kaballah before taking a step back. "I can do this to you all night."

Bolan believed that she could, but he wasn't convinced the fight was knocked out of the terrorist. Rage and hate still burned in the man's eyes. The Executioner looked at Yerzim, who was sitting comfortably in his chair, smoking, looking as if he didn't have a care in the world. Then Yerzim fixed Bolan with a narrow-eyed gaze, shaking his head, silently telling the Executioner not to interfere.

Without warning, the terrorist sprung at Weisskopf, clawed hands going for her throat. The woman exploded through Kaballah's arms, knocking them aside, then head-butted the terrorist. There was a sickening squelch of bone, and blood sprayed from Kaballah's pulped nose like a burst faucet. The Iraqi slumped to the floor.

Weisskopf descended on the terrorist, locking an arm around his throat, grabbing one arm and wrenching it up behind his back, giving the terrorist all the lift he needed to stand. The Iraqi struggled, his eyes bulging in pain and fear, but Weisskopf wrenched on his arm and Kaballah froze in her grasp.

"Do you talk?" the woman grated in Kaballah's ear. "I can start by breaking your arm. Your neck would be next."

"Okay, okay," the Iraqi sputtered. "I will talk."

Weisskopf put more pressure on the terrorist's arm, raising a cry of pain, then whirled and pushed the man onto the couch. For long moments Kaballah hacked, rubbing his throat, his eyes glazed as he tried to compose himself.

"This gentleman behind me," Weisskopf told the Iraqi, jerking a nod at Bolan, "is an American. You and your animals have killed many of his people on their own soil. I'm sure you remember the attack just outside the United Nations Building in New York City by your brother Iraqis now imprisoned by us. Should you not talk to me, I will turn you over to him. Since I know he has not forgotten the attacks that killed many of his people, I have a feeling he will show you far less mercy than I have."

Bolan watched Kaballah as the terrorist looked up at him. Fear shadowed the Iraqi's face before he quickly broke the Executioner's steely gaze.

"I said I would talk," Kaballah growled. "You are three, you have the guns. But your day will come and—"

Suddenly Weisskopf whipped out her Walther. Kaballah shrieked as the Walther cracked a round that drilled into the divan. Stuffing exploded from between Kaballah's legs.

"Start with the Mossad agent you claimed has helped you," Weisskopf demanded.

Kaballah hesitated, then, as the woman aimed the Walther at his groin, the terrorist blurted, "Baumstein. His name is Baumstein. Yes, one of your own has betrayed you."

Bolan saw the instant change on the faces of both Mossad agents as Yerzim and Weisskopf locked eyes. It was as if the life were being sucked right out of them.

"Damn," Yerzim breathed. "Baumstein."

Kaballah coughed, wincing as he tried to gather composure. "Yes, your Mossad man, Baumstein. He gave us all the necessary papers—passports, identification. He gave us safehouses and even kept Mossad off our backs, steering your people in other directions. It was just our bad luck that he couldn't protect Aziz and the others."

An expression of murder hardened Weisskopf's face when Kaballah announced that piece of bad luck with obvious regret. Her eyes started to close with this knowledge of betrayal, then she laid full and savage attention on the terrorist.

Bolan asked Yerzim, "Where is this Baumstein? How important is he?"

"Baumstein was sent by Mossad to interrogate Kamal at the prison compound," Yerzim stated. "He is a top man in Mossad. He is a very important counterterrorist agent."

"The traitorous bastard," Weisskopf snarled under her breath.

"Yeah, well, this counterterrorist agent is holding Kamal's hand," Bolan said. "We can be sure now

there'll be an attack. This Baumstein is keeping whoever will attack the compound informed. He probably has access to long-range radio communication with
whoever is going to try and break Kamal out. Meaning they'll know my country is on the way to get
Kamal and when they'll be landing on the Sinai."

"Why?" Yerzim barked at Kaballah. "Why did
Baumstein do it?"

"For money, what else?" Kaballah said, as if Yerzim had asked a stupid question. Then the terrorist
laughed strangely. "Six months ago I was in Berlin.
That is where this nightmare of you Jews all started."

"We already know that," Weisskopf said. "You
exploded a car that killed more than twenty people,"

Kaballah shrugged, then smiled, smug.

"You already told us about Tiel and Mauser,"
Weisskopf added, then turned to Bolan.

"One was Red Army trash, the other was a former
GSG-9 man who turned on his own people and joined
the Red Army. Again, I suspect he did it for the
money. Both were being sought by Interpol after the
attack in Berlin but both have disappeared. This one
told us they joined Aziz and his people, worked an
arms deal through various Russian contacts the former GSG-9 man had, but this GSG-9 man didn't have
the money, apparently. That, Kaballah has informed
us, is when another man entered the deal."

The woman returned grim attention to the terrorist. "Tell us about this 'merchandise' that is going to

be delivered to you and your friends," Weisskopf demanded. "Tell us who is in charge of the strike force that is going to attempt to free Kamal."

Kaballah looked pointedly at Bolan and laughed. "The man who will free Aziz, he is one of your own. He is a former CIA man. His name is Robert Gorman." The Iraqi paused to let it sink in. "I have seen this man and I can tell you he is completely insane. He is a vision of the devil in human skin, and he has much money. Gorman is well armed and well equipped. Yes, he will free Aziz."

Bolan felt the stares of the Mossad agents boring into him.

"You know this man, Mr. Belasko?" Yerzim asked. "This Robert Gorman of the CIA?"

"I've heard of him," Bolan admitted. "When I was in Vietnam, it was rumored he was a black-market profiteer running guns and drugs. He ran clandestine operations for the CIA into Cambodia and Laos. Had a team of dirty soldiers under his command that called themselves Phantom Force. Gorman was never caught doing his dirty work, but he hurt and killed a lot of people on both sides."

"He worked for the CIA," Weisskopf reminded.

"A lot of people worked for the CIA. Gorman would have been what the Company calls one of their 'animals,' a paramilitary operative. He was a mercenary, an assassin, doing the wet work, all the dirty jobs the CIA has done but no one ever reads about in the papers. If Gorman's behind the impending breakout of Kamal—''

"He is," Kaballah interrupted.

"Then we've got problems," Bolan said. "Gorman would have the money, the contacts and the firepower to pull it off."

"The merchandise," Weisskopf asked Kaballah.

"That was something that was done between Tiel, Mauser, Aziz and Gorman," the Iraqi answered. "I was never part of the arms deal. I only know it involved some sort of missiles."

"Could be anything," Yerzim said. "Air to air, surface to air, antitank."

"They could also be nuclear-armed missiles," Weisskopf added.

"I know that Gorman got what Aziz wanted," Kaballah said. "The deal went down in Syria. Gorman took Tiel and Mauser and several of our own people to meet with the Russian agents. There was a good deal of money involved, tens of millions, I understand. The Russians apparently wanted more money, but Gorman did not have it. Gorman killed the Russians and took what he wanted."

Bolan felt his blood run hot with anger. One thing he couldn't tolerate in any situation was a traitor.

"I need to get in touch with Colonel Yoraam, warn him about Baumstein and have him arrested," Yerzim stated.

"No," Bolan said. "Play it like we don't know anything. Get us to the Sinai compound. You can handle Baumstein there. Any advanced warning of what we know—well, there could be others working with Baumstein. If Gorman is tipped off, he could move sooner than I'd like."

Yerzim didn't seem to like the idea of Bolan taking charge. "You seem to place great confidence in yourself to be able to handle this entire situation, Mr. Belasko."

"My country wouldn't have sent me otherwise, Mr. Yerzim. How long would it take to arrange a flight for me to the Sinai compound?"

"I can have it done within the hour," Weisskopf replied. "It may take a little longer, but I can have you there within four hours tops."

"Let's get moving," Bolan said.

"I will escort you two back to Mossad headquarters," Weisskopf said. "But my business here is not finished."

She looked coldly at Kaballah. "You and I still have a lot to talk about. Alone."

Kaballah laughed. "You three are fools if you think you can stop what has already been set in motion."

"I will tell you this much," Weisskopf said. "If one more Israeli dies while you are in my custody, I will personally kill you on the spot."

The Iraqi didn't look so smug anymore. Okay, Bolan thought, Mossad still had cockroaches in Israel to flush out and crush, and the Iraqi had just tasted firsthand the deadly serious business that the lady agent was all about.

As he led the·Israelis to the door, a grim and foreboding feeling nagged him. If what the terrorist had told them was true, and Bolan had no reason to doubt what he'd heard, the Executioner suspected all hell was going to break loose in the Sinai Desert.

UNITED STATES SPECIAL Forces Colonel Mike Marlin was tired, worried and felt every bit his fifty-two years of age. Feeling the vibrations of the C-130's turboprop engines rattling through him, the hum of those powerful engines filling his ears with an eerie muting, Marlin knew he was in danger of remembering that time in Vietnam. The colonel clenched his teeth, squeezed his eyes shut and felt the hate boil up deep from in his belly.

For long moments he seethed in silence. Then somehow he steeled himself, fought off those visions of his past hell, knowing he could lose all perspective on his present mission if he thought about the past and focused himself solely on vengeance. But if the man who had shattered his life so long ago was somewhere in the Middle East, Marlin would fight the forces of heaven, hell and earth to find and to kill him. With sheer willpower he resisted the temptation of reaching into his pocket and pulling out their photo.

The colonel stood and looked at the force of thirty young soldiers he commanded. They were sitting aft in the gunship, hard, determined faces sheened by the ghostly glow of overhead lights. Some of them were asleep; some were cleaning their M-17s; others smoked or drank coffee. Three of those soldiers were killing time by playing cards. The colonel knew all of them were anxious to land in the Sinai Desert and pick up the Iraqi terrorists, whisk them back to the States where they would stand trial and most certainly be thrown away for a lifetime in prison, courtesy of Uncle Sam.

Suddenly, as was happening more lately, Colonel Marlin felt the pain in his stomach rip through him like hot, twisting knives, making him wince. Again he dredged up the strength of pure will, this time to keep from doubling over.

As he stood beneath the soft glow of light, Marlin's gaunt face looked ghostly, and the intense pain he felt contorted his face into a mask of agony. A moment later he found himself looking at his soldiers, hoping none of them noticed how much pain he was in. For damn sure, he knew he looked like walking death, but there was good reason for that. Colonel Mike Marlin was dying.

In just one year the colonel's hair had turned from iron gray to stock white. What fire that used to burn in his bright blue eyes was now doused by the look of dull anger, the eyes now sunken pools in a sharp but shriveled face that looked like a death's-head. His weight was down from one-eighty to one-fifty, and there were moments when the 9 mm Beretta holstered on his hip felt like a great weight.

The doctors had told him the cancer in his stomach was too far along, and they had given him about six months. What seemed strange to the colonel was that the top brass knew all about his terminal condition, which made him wonder why he'd been given command of this mission in the first place. Was it out of respect for one of America's most decorated war heroes, or was it sympathy? Whichever it was, he was determined to insure the world's most notorious terrorist was picked up and turned over to the appropriate authorities to face justice. But that didn't mean Marlin was going back to the States. Yeah, there was another, more personal reason why he wanted to go to the Middle East.

The colonel stared past his troops at the three men hunched over maps to the rear of the gunship. They were the three CIA goons, Crueller, Thomson and Jackel. Marlin detested having the CIA leeched onto this mission, but the top brass had ordered him to cooperate. Supposedly those three were going to the Sinai to interrogate Kamal in the interests of national security. Since leaving Andrews Air Force Base, the three agents hadn't said a word to him, but he now needed to have a talk with one of them in the worst way. When Marlin had earlier glimpsed their maps of the Middle East, he had also seen a photo of his most hated enemy.

Fighting the terrible pain in his stomach, holding his expression into a stony mask of grim determination, the colonel felt the eyes of his troops locked on to him as he walked up to the CIA men.

Crueller looked up from Marlin's shadow on his intelligence files, a flicker of irritation crossing the man's face. Marlin ran a hard stare over the three agents, silently letting them know he was in a no-nonsense mood. He wondered for a moment why the three agents seemed to look the same. It was as if their physical appearance and garb were some sort of prerequisite for the job. All three men were lean six-footers in their late thirties, with chiseled-granite faces. They were dressed in black, toting 9 mm Glock pistols in shoulder holsters. All had closely cropped hair and the same sort of dead stare in their eyes where the only life that shone was a hint of anger, or perhaps cunning, once in a while.

Marlin had seen their ilk too many times during and after Vietnam. They were the grim reapers harvesting more death in the guise of freedom and democracy, the shadow players who fomented turmoil and unrest and profited from the suffering of others. No, Colonel Marlin didn't like them, not one damn bit.

"Can I help you, Colonel?" Crueller asked.

"I want to talk to you. Alone."

The colonel ran his hard stare over the three agents again, then wheeled and strode past his troops. Glancing back over his shoulder, Marlin saw Crueller throw Thomson and Jackel a weary look. Finally the CIA man stood and followed the colonel amidships.

When he knew they were far enough away from all ears, Marlin told Crueller, "I want to know if your people have found him. And if you have, what it is you intend to do with him."

Crueller cleared his throat. "Colonel, I know all about what happened to you in Vietnam. When you say 'him,' I assume you're speaking of Robert Gorman?"

"Who the hell else would I be talking about, mister?"

"Look, I know all about the allegations you made against Gorman, how you suspected him of murdering your family and of almost killing you. It's all in my files."

"Your files don't tell you that it was always more than just suspicion with me," Marlin said. "If you knew this man like I did, you wouldn't be so, uh, cavalier about my past. What you don't know about Gorman and me you'll never read in your files."

Crueller stiffened with sudden anger. "Colonel, we have an extremely important mission to perform for our country. Your vengeance isn't part of our agenda. For your information, my files on you and on Gorman are a whole lot more detailed and complete than you think. For instance, I know you went after this man in Vietnam, on your own. You played the crusader role once and lost. Fact is, you made a lot of noise to the top brass back then about Gormàn and his so-called Phantom Force. What they found back then, a hundred years ago in a war no one but guys like you remember anymore, was a bunch of Vietcong across the border in Cambodia, running the guns-and-drugs operation you claimed Gorman was directing. Need I go on?''

The colonel had ice in his voice as he said, ''Let me tell you something that you won't find in your files, and that is that certain factions within the CIA created men like Robert Gorman in Vietnam. Both to prolong the war and make a profit from the illicit drugs-and-arms trade. I could never prove it, no, but I am one hundred percent certain that it was Robert Gorman who pumped a half-dozen slugs into me from a safe distance in the dead of a rainy night in the jungles of Cambodia, and I am just as certain he either killed or gave the orders for murders of my wife and son in Saigon.

''Further, I also believe the CIA covered his ass and helped Gorman to disappear after the war. Meaning I neither like nor trust you or anything that stinks of the CIA. And if you don't give me the answers I want, straight answers, I'll toss you and your lackeys off this plane from twenty thousand feet up with no parachute. I need your help like I need the pain I've got in my stomach."

Crueller peered at the cold fury in Marlin's eyes, then nodded, appearing unfazed by the man's threat. "Okay, Colonel. Fire away. What do you want to know?"

"We both know that there is the possibility of an attack to free Kamal. I don't give a damn if it is just a rumor by some wild-ass terrorist thugs. During my briefing at the Pentagon, when your people from Langley were present, the name Gorman came up four times. Rumor—Gorman has put together a mercenary army that may or may not attempt to free Kamal. Rumor—no one knows where the guy is or what exactly he's planned. My suspicion—somebody knows something they're not telling me. Since I'm the commanding officer of this convoy, I want you to tell me what you know."

Crueller's thin lips parted in a smile that looked as if it belonged more on a reptile than a human being.

"Here it is, Colonel, point-blank. We have people in that part of the world who have both spotted Gorman and have worked undercover to bring him in. Gorman, as you well know, is one tough, smart bastard, well armed, well-informed. Our agents were compromised, but not before we learned of an arms deal that turned sour in Syria, a deal between Kamal, Gorman and some former KGB agents, the old-line guard, hard-core Stalinists who were none too happy

with the new Russia. Our sources in Syria informed us
the arms deal went off, but Gorman got what he
wanted by the barrel of his gun. And I'm not talking
about a crate of grenades or AKs. I'm talking serious
high-tech hardware, nuclear hardware, in fact. What
and where this hardware is, we don't know at this
point.

"Yes, we do believe Gorman has put together a
strike force that may or may not attempt to free
Kamal. My mission is to interrogate Kamal about
Gorman's whereabouts or the whereabouts of any of
Kamal's flunkies who are still running around with
Gorman.

"I don't care if I have to slap Kamal silly or attach
electrodes to his balls and fire him up with enough
juice to fry him clear into hell. I want the rest of
Kamal's thugs who are still out there, I want Gorman
and I want what Gorman is sitting on. That's my mission—that's both straight from Langley and the Pentagon. And you, Colonel, are expected to cooperate
with me fully."

"You still haven't answered my original question."

"When I find Gorman, Colonel, I intend to termi-
nate him with extreme prejudice."

"What if you don't get to him first?"

"Just what is that supposed to mean?" When
Marlin didn't answer, Crueller continued, "Colonel,
I am warning you, this mission isn't about something
that happened between you and Gorman more than

twenty years ago. Your superiors wouldn't take kindly to any interference with my mission.''

"Believe me, I don't intend to interfere."

Crueller peered at Marlin for several stretched seconds as if searching for some way to enhance his threat.

"If you'll excuse me, Colonel, I've got work to do. I suggest you get some rest. You don't look so good.''

Marlin allowed the guy his parting shot, watched Crueller spin on his heel and head back to his maps and files. The colonel then saw some of his troops watching him. They were aware something was wrong, he knew, but they didn't know how wrong things were.

And something was very seriously wrong. The CIA man wasn't telling the colonel everything he knew, nor would he. Whatever the agents decided to do had to be right and just—because it was done in the name of freedom. It was the same way his personal vengeance hunt against Gorman had been handled by the CIA and his superiors so long ago. Colonel Marlin had seen a little too much in his life to fall for that double-standard crap, the "us-and-them syndrome," he had come to call it.

A strange, haunted feeling suddenly descended over Marlin. He took a seat in the shadows, alone. He told himself not to do it, started to reach into his pocket, then froze. Suddenly he felt disembodied, beyond and above it all.

The images exploded in his mind against his will, a jumbled maze of horrible memories that had been tormenting him for more than twenty years. He saw six soldiers under his command, all of them acting on their own, shot to hell, lying in the mud on the jungle floor, their eyes wide in death. The ambush had come out of nowhere, it seemed.

Lightning was flashing, illuminating the jungle around him, but through the downpour Marlin couldn't see who it was who had sniped them off. There was a hooch at the end of the trail, and Marlin was retreating for the cover it provided. Marlin then saw himself falling. He recalled the pain, that fire racing through his body, which told him he was being shot up.

Then, as he lay in the mud, he saw the figure step out of the brush. He couldn't be certain it was Gorman, because the figure had painted his face black, and the haze of mind-numbing agony was fading to a dark curtain of impending shock. But Marlin would never forget those eyes. They were blue eyes that looked inhuman, eyes that seemed to burn with hate and anger.

Marlin saw the M-16 lift in the demon's hand, then sputter its lead flame. Then everything turned black. And there he was, in a hospital bed, floating on a cloud of morphine. Doctors told him they had dug out six bullets, all of them just missing vital parts. A Special Forces recon team had found him less than an hour after the ambush.

The image faded. Marlin fought to keep himself from seeing it, but he couldn't help it. It lived in his mind, so fresh, so vivid it was as if it had only happened yesterday. He shuddered, felt the cry of anguish rip from deep in his belly as he saw Chan Li and their son, Peter, lying in their villa six months later. Their faces were shattered from the bullets that had been pumped through their head, and the note on his wife's chest had been scrawled in her blood.

Marlin squeezed his eyes shut, holding back the flood of tears he felt building from deep within him. He had loved her and their son more than anything in life. No, they had been his life. All those years since, he had felt like a living dead man, detached and unattached from everything and everyone except for his work as an officer. He'd never been able to prove his suspicions. There'd been no answers from anybody, no help. No leads.

The damn guy seemed to have just disappeared off the face of the earth.

Until now.

Marlin opened his eyes and looked at the CIA goons. They weren't about to tell him a damn thing more about Gorman. But if the bastard who had destroyed his life was in the Middle East . . .

The colonel thought the unthinkable. With only six months to live, he wasn't going back to the States. Life had kicked the crap out of him, handed him a raw deal, but he was going out like a lion. Colonel Mike Marlin was going to find and kill Robert Gorman even if it was the last thing he did on earth. Vengeance was all he had left.

4

"That's it, people—lock and load. We're airborne in five minutes," Gorman announced. "Our pigeons are about to land. And let me tell you, you had damn well better have your heads right for this. Now, listen up. I have one last thing to say to you."

Except for his two six-man ground-assault teams, one led by Collins, the other by Crocker, Gorman's army was gathered in the main tent for the final briefing. The Mil Mi-6 helicopter had just returned from off-loading his ground-assault force, so Gorman knew those strike teams were in place, his best men out there in the desert less than four klicks from the prison compound. One team was to move in under the cover of darkness, waiting until exactly 0430 to begin the assault while the "trailer team" waited at a distance for the air assault to begin. Then they would go in and add to what would hopefully only be a mop-up operation.

Gorman stood before his troops, hands on his hips, giving his men a long, hard look, sizing them up, unable to keep from wondering who would live and who would die. For damn sure, he knew there would be those who wouldn't collect on a one-hundred-grand payday, which meant just a little more cash in his pocket. D day, Death day, had arrived.

Mentally he did a quick assessment of his fire and manpower. First he had a small army of some of the best-trained ex-military men in the world, now battle-hardened mercenaries driven by bloodlust and propelled by greed to live. Second, and most important, he had a half-dozen of the most formidable attack helicopters ever produced, six Mil Mi-24s and the lone Mi-6, which would peel off and wait in the desert until the strike was over before ordered to land on the compound's perimeter and load their principals.

Each Mi-24 carried a 12.7 mm machine gun in the nose, with 32-round packs of 57 mm rockets. Add four "Swatter" homing antitank missiles on the wingtip launchers, and he knew he had the finest scourge of death from above. As the Soviets had proved in their war against the *mujahadin* in Afghanistan, those gunships were invulnerable against small-arms fire, thanks to the gunship's steel-and-titanium hull. Once again Gorman owed his old KGB buddies a debt of gratitude for getting him the aircraft. Too bad they would never collect what they were owed.

His gaze swept over his men, and he had to wonder whether Julius Caesar felt as pumped up before addressing his Roman legions on the eve of battle. Hell, he thought, when this was over, he would be a veritable twentieth-century conqueror. Either way, he was going to make history. Fortune was sweeter when it also had fame attached to it.

The mercenary leader looked ghoulish and menacing as he stood in the soft yellow light that flickered from a kerosene lamp. Reuter sat behind him, puffing on a foot long cigar, studying the hard crew with the same grim stare as his boss.

"Gorman's Law is now in effect," the big man told his troops, "and Gorman's Law is this—if something will go wrong, take care of it by wearing Godzilla-sized balls. Kill any and all of the enemy. Show no mercy, take no prisoners. I do not intend to leave anyone breathing other than us. When we leave this compound, I want everything dead. I want to see everything destroyed and burned to the ground. I want it to be a vision of hell, and I want it to put the fear of God into anyone who thinks they've got the stones to come after us. D day stands for Death day, people."

He let that sink in as he scoured their faces. Gorman spotted the usual prebattle jitters in their eyes. Fear. But fear was good, if channeled into action. He was getting more pumped by the minute, imagined he could almost smell the adrenaline in the air.

"You people are seasoned pros, you know the drill. Get in hard, fuck 'em up harder, and out hardest, last and only. Now, you know that some of you might not be coming back to collect your hundred grand. But if you take Gorman's Law to heart, you'll live and you'll earn more money in one day than you'll ever see again working for some shitty clandestine government-sanctioned operation in a no-name Third World, third-rate country no one gives a damn about anyway.

"Now, one final matter. I've touched on this, but I will go into greater detail later. All I'm prepared to say at this point is once we leave that compound behind, with our principals in tow, phase two begins. Phase two is our main goal. I will continue to need your services in order to complete phase two. Those who cooperate and help me complete phase two will get an additional twenty-thousand-dollar bonus."

Gorman gave them one last penetrating stare. "Get your gear. And remember Gorman's Law. Dismissed. Good luck and good killing."

Feeling like a proud father, Gorman watched them stand and gather their weapons. As they filed out of the tent, he liked what he saw on their faces. Each and every one of them looked grim with determination, ready to kill. Yeah, they knew the drill and they looked ready to take his instructions to heart.

When they were alone, Gorman looked at Reuter as his right-hand man stood. A flicker of concern in the man's eyes soured his mood a little.

"Something bothering you?"

"If our man in place doesn't take care of radar and radio communication, well, then *Murphy's* Law will be in effect."

"I gave him the most-sophisticated high-tech electronic radar and radio-jamming device available," Gorman stated, noticing that Reuter was now puffing a little nervously on his stogie. "Another gift, straight from my Russian buddies who dropped a twenty-million-dollar payday in our laps. That Russian Sphinx box will work. All he has to do is turn it on. It'll cut off the entire compound from any communication to the outside world. It'll be like the lights have been turned off just before the sky falls on their heads. Just before we trample them into the dirt. Look, if their radar was working, our Mi-6 wouldn't have returned. Right?"

"Maybe. But what if he gets cold feet or they've found him out?"

"Then Gorman's Law is still in effect. If it happens we come under fire because he didn't do his job, I'll leave him a broken, bloody corpse for the buzzards before we evacuate. And if you're worried about those bedouin being there in the wadi to meet Crocker and the others, don't. I made a deal with the Arab myself. Ten grand will buy that desert rat a whole lot of good times in Cairo. Guy believes in old Ben Franklin a whole lot more than he does Allah. That's why he hasn't been paid until he gives our people what I'm paying for. Anything else?"

Reuter shook his head, dropped the stogie and ground it out beneath his heel. He showed Gorman a mean smile, then chuckled. "I especially liked the part about Godzilla-sized balls."

"Well, I wasn't looking for laughs," Gorman said coldly.

Reuter paused, seeming to choose his next words carefully. "I didn't see anyone laughing."

"Let's go earn twenty million bucks," Gorman said. "Then we can laugh all the way to a Swiss bank."

He cast Reuter one last piercing look, then blew out the light.

COLONEL YORAAM WAS striding across the compound to find out just what had happened to their radar and communications system when he heard a faint rumbling in the distance. He stopped cold, searching the black sky. A moment later he pinpointed the rumble to the north, the sound of thunder growing louder with each passing second.

Sergeant Eitan, right on the colonel's heels, stopped abruptly, worry etching his face.

"I don't understand it, Colonel. Our entire radar and radio systems just shut down. There's no apparent malfunction that we can find. I've got a crew on it now, sir, we'll find the problem and have everything working again."

"Is there a problem, Colonel?" another voice asked.

Yoraam saw Baumstein striding toward him from the direction of the Land Rovers. He ignored the

Mossad man, searching the compound then the surrounding desert. Everything felt terribly wrong, and Yoraam began to fear the worst. Klieg lights washed the entire compound and perimeter. Light burned out into the desert in all directions, but began to fade before hitting total darkness at about a hundred meters. Another string of klieg lights lit up a stretch of desert to the east where the Americans would land.

Yoraam believed the rumble he heard was the thunder of the American C-130. But now he wasn't sure of anything. The desert seemed ominously still and quiet beyond the light. It always felt like that right before it hit the fan. Perhaps an hour ago, just about the time when their radar had mysteriously shut down, the colonel had been informed by one of his men that he thought he had heard a helicopter in the distance. Without radar, it was impossible to tell what, if anything, was out there. Yoraam couldn't spare the time or manpower right now for a recon of the desert.

As Baumstein halted in front of Yoraam, the colonel, looking skyward with an intense gaze, said, "I strongly suspect someone has sabotaged our radar and communications. We are now, in effect, cut off from the world."

"Sabotage?" Eitan said. "But who? How?"

"You have proof of this, Colonel?" Baumstein asked.

Yoraam looked the Mossad agent dead in the eye. In that moment he caught just enough of something dangerous flickering through Baumstein's eyes that warned him to watch his back.

"No, Mr. Baumstein, I do not have proof. When I do, you will be the first to know."

Baumstein kept up his hard front. "What does that mean, Colonel?"

"It means what it means," Yoraam stated, then returned his attention skyward.

A finger of white light traced the sky as the thunder rolled over the compound. Moments later, as Yoraam watched the searching beam, the dark shape of the behemoth C-130 was hit by the light. He saw his soldiers racing to secure the landing strip, the row of lights flashing out on the desert floor. The transport began angling for the runway.

"Sergeant," Yoraam said, "secure the perimeter with four four-man fireteams, north, south, east and west. Break out the Stingers and the RPGs."

Eitan looked confused. "Sir, that would be the Americans coming in."

"Yes, it would, Sergeant, and, no, I don't intend to blow them out of the sky. It isn't the Americans I'm worried about."

Eitan moved out. Yoraam watched as the C-130 landed, then rolled down the runway, kicking up a huge funnel of dust in its thundering wake. Suddenly Eitan was back.

"Sir, we've got movement to the northwest. Looks like another clan of bedouin."

Yoraam peered in that direction. Indeed, moving slowly from the veil of darkness and into the outer reaches of light, the colonel spotted six figures on camelback. Suddenly there was too much movement, too much mystery, too much happening at one time, all of it now coming in on the wings of weeks of rumor and speculation. Yoraam felt prebattle adrenaline burst through his veins.

"So, send someone out there," he told Eitan. "If he gives you any trouble, have him detained. Get moving!"

"Sir, I don't have anyone available at the moment. They're either putting shackles on the prisoners, working to get the radar and radio working again or securing the—"

"Then do it yourself, Sergeant. After you've secured the perimeter with the fireteams, take two men and go out there."

"Yes, sir," Eitan said, spinning on his heel and marching off.

"Colonel, I demand to know what is going on," Baumstein said. "You act as if we are about to be attacked."

Yoraam headed for the runway. Again he ignored the Mossad man but felt Baumstein's stare boring into the back of his head.

"Colonel?"

"I didn't say we're going to be attacked, Mr. Baumstein, did I?"

Yoraam closed on the C-130, saw figures wearing berets and toting M-16s disembark from the aircraft. His paranoia mounting, he felt compelled to strike out at something, anything, but there was no visible or known threat at the moment.

With his intense gaze focused solely on his men scrambling around the compound to carry out his orders, the Israeli was aware of nothing else until he heard, "You must be Colonel Yoraam. I'm Colonel Mike Marlin, United States Special Forces. Pleased to meet you, Colonel."

Yoraam returned the American officer's salute. He thought he saw Marlin wince, then wondered if maybe the look wasn't an expression of anger. Either way, the man appeared ill, as pale as a ghost in the lights of the runway. The Israeli felt embarrassed that he thought Marlin didn't look fit for duty.

"Colonel Yoraam, is something wrong with your communications system here? We've been trying to radio you for the past twenty minutes."

BOLAN KNEW something was wrong. He sat alone in the belly of the CH-53, with rotor wash whipping through the open fuselage doorway, listening to Yerzim again order the pilot to try to raise the compound by radio.

"It's no use, sir," the pilot replied. "Nothing but static."

"Keep trying."

Bolan read the fear on Yerzim's face as the man moved from the cockpit to stand in the doorway and stare at the desert floor, five hundred feet below the chopper. He gave the Israeli a few moments to digest what the Executioner already knew—the attack to free Kamal was either underway or it was going to happen at any time.

The big American used the silence to chew over his recent talk with Brognola. The big Fed's update still rang with ominous overtones. He had informed Bolan that a decorated Vietnam War hero, Colonel Mike Marlin on Special Forces, was in command of the team sent to pick up Kamal. Bolan didn't know the man personally, but he'd heard of Marlin. And from what he had heard about the man, he suspected there weren't too many finer fighting men to come out of that war.

Bolan had also been told about the past between Marlin and Gorman, from the ambush in Cambodia, where Marlin had survived six bullets, right up to when the man had found his Vietnamese wife and their son shot to death in their Saigon villa. It had happened only months after Marlin had gotten out of the hospital and was about to be shipped back to the States. It was on record, Brognola had informed Bolan, that Marlin always believed Gorman was responsible for the attempt on his life and the murders of his wife and son. It was also on record that Marlin always suspected a faction of the CIA of running a black-market drugs-and-guns operation in Laos and Cambodia and that Gorman had run that operation. Except for the rumor of a CIA connection, there was nothing Brognola could dig up about Gorman after the Vietnam War. It was as if the guy had vanished into thin air.

There it was, Bolan thought. Nothing had ever been proved about Gorman's activities during the war. In fact, top brass had appeared to sweep any rumors or suspicions about Gorman under the rug, which told the Executioner that someone high up had been protecting him. As for Marlin, well, he had returned home—with a chest full of medals and ribbons, with bitter memories and nights full of bad dreams—to apparently live a quiet if not tormented life, Bolan believed. That Marlin had been chosen to command this convoy was somewhat strange to Bolan, since Brognola seemed to think the man was retired.

Further, Brognola had told Bolan the CIA was in on the act, tagging along with Marlin to interrogate Kamal and his brothers in terrorism. Bolan was both puzzled and troubled by this new information. Supposedly Gorman had been a CIA paramilitary operative gone renegade for reasons unknown, greed most likely. It was believed the man had more money than most Third World countries, and had allegedly made that fortune off guns, drugs and murder. And finally Gorman had a suspicious past in Special Forces in Vietnam, where he had honed his cutthroat blade be-

fore allegedly moving on to other things while working for the CIA.

The only clear fact Bolan could put into the scenario was that Gorman and Marlin could be on the
verge of crossing paths. Most certainly only one of
them would walk away. Coincidence? Or was someone jerking the strings on Marlin for reasons unknown? Was Gorman getting help from someone in
the CIA to put together this breakout and the impending arms deal? Or did the CIA want Gorman
terminated with extreme prejudice to cover its own
sins, to eliminate a national embarrassment?

Whatever was going on with the other players,
whatever was ahead for any of them, Bolan knew his
mission was unchanged.

It was still open season on any of Kamal's terrorists who were out there and might attempt to reset foot
on American soil.

Still, Robert Gorman was bad news. The man was
a predator Bolan intended to put to sleep forever if and
when their paths crossed.

Yerzim laid a grim eye on Bolan. "I don't know
how he did it, but I'd bet my last bullet Baumstein
somehow sabotaged their radar and communications
network. He belongs to me."

"I don't have any problem with that. How long before we reach the compound?"

"We're almost there," Yerzim answered, picking up
an Uzi subgun, ejecting the clip, checking its load,

then slapping the clip home. "Less than five minutes, according to our pilot."

Like the Israeli, Bolan was now dressed in combat black. His Beretta 93-R was holstered in shoulder leather, with the .44 Magnum Desert Eagle riding on his hip. The Uzi submachine gun he had requested earlier lay on the bench beside him. Six spare clips for the Uzi, with an equal number of clips for both the Beretta and the big .44, hung on his military webbing.

Suddenly the pilot turned toward Yerzim. "Sir, I've got something on radar on the ground. One o'clock, about two klicks ahead."

Bolan and Yerzim were no sooner at the door than the Mossad agent was handing the Executioner one of two infrared binoculars. A moment later Bolan spotted an object at the exact point where the pilot had mentioned. In a gulley that spined through a low chain of hills, the transport truck was clearly outlined in the greenish red tunnel vision of Bolan's binoculars.

"If I didn't know better, that looks like a Russian transport truck to me," Yerzim stated. "Swing it south, mister," Yerzim ordered the pilot. "I'll tell you when to hover."

"I'm not sure sure that's a good idea, Yerzim," Bolan said, lowering the binoculars, then moving to the bench to grab his Uzi. "If that's Gorman or some of his men and they've got rocket firepower, the Sinai could end up our graveyard."

Both the pilot and the copilot were looking over their shoulders at Bolan and Yerzim, obviously having heard the exchange and waiting to see if the Mossad agent changed his orders. Yerzim looked through the binoculars again.

"They're heading out of the wadi, and it looks to me like they're going straight toward the compound. Fly us to the end of that gulley," Yerzim ordered the pilot, "then set it down. I want them cut off."

Bolan didn't like it. His combat senses were on full alert as the chopper veered south, then began sweeping over the southern rim of jagged peaks. Again Bolan took in the gully through his binoculars as they passed the transport truck. He spotted a man poking his head out of the passenger's side and glimpsed the muzzle of an assault rifle. Those guys down there were the enemy, Bolan knew, and they were hell-bent on fighting it out. But this play wasn't his call. Bolan braced himself for the worst, prepared to move in an eye blink with lethal intent.

"Hit that truck with a searchlight," Yerzim ordered the pilot. "We'll make the approach on foot. If they open fire, you lift off and blow them out of this wadi."

Bolan tensed as the chopper lowered into the mouth of the gulley. A huge cloud of dust was kicked up by rotor wash, the searchlight stabbing through the swirling wall of grit and pinning the transport truck, which suddenly stopped.

"Come on," Yerzim told Bolan, leaping out of the doorway as the chopper touched down.

Just as Bolan hit the ground, he saw the first flashes of weapons fire, heard the tracking line of slugs whining off the chopper's fuselage. Knowing they were exposed to the enemy, Bolan grabbed Yerzim and dragged him to cover behind a boulder. As autofire chattered and the hellstorm of lead pounded their position, the Executioner looked back and saw the chopper start to lift off to get out of the line of fire. The Israeli chopper's searchlight raked the sky, and Bolan spotted the dark shapes of seven helicopter gunships bearing down on the gulley, coming in nose-down from the west. He knew the Israeli flyboys were doomed.

CROCKER PULLED the *kaffiyeh* tight to his face. Even from a hundred yards out, he could feel the tension at the compound, saw a dozen soldiers scrambling to take up defensive positions around the perimeter, toting what appeared to be rocket launchers. Did they know about the attack? he wondered. Hell, they sure looked as if they were on full alert.

He took in the scene with mounting fear and anger. It looked as though the American convoy was already there, just as Gorman had told them it would be. Green Berets and Israeli soldiers were either gathered around the C-130 or heading straight for a building that Crocker knew from his final briefing was the prison holding their principals. But what was really happening? he wondered, then looked at Hammersmith, who sat atop the camel next to him, the man's dark eyes burning with the same fear and anger just above the *kaffiyeh* drawn across his face.

Damn, Crocker thought, checking the illuminated dial of his watch. It was 0430 hours. He strained his ears for the sound of rotor blades. Gorman and his gunship armada were supposed to be coming in from the west at that very moment, and Collins and his team would be on the way, coming in for the attack on the compound from the north side. Everything was supposed to be synchronized for a simultaneous ground and air assault.

Crocker saw the Land Rover breaking from the compound, heading their way. Nothing to do but wait, he told himself, nothing to do but hold on and put his faith in Gorman's Law.

So far Gorman's Law had worked. It had been a good hour's hard ride from the wadi where the bedouin had been paid for the camels, robes and headgear the team now wore. The bedouin had done well, his Intel to Gorman about the compound accurate and complete. Most importantly, aside from numbers and layout, the bedouin had said someone would ride out and tell them to get away from the secured area.

Crocker drew a deep breath, slid his arm up the sleeve of his robe and clamped a fist over his Uzi subgun. He knew he couldn't wait much longer.

"They're late," Hammersmith stated.

"They'll be here." Crocker watched the Land Rover head straight for them, pinning the six of them in the glare of the headlights as it quickly cut the distance.

5

Bolan returned fire with his Uzi, his tracking line of 9 mm slugs shattering the windshield of the transport truck. Behind the implosion of glass, the Executioner caught a glimpse of the driver clutching his bloodied and tattered chest before tumbling from the door. A heartbeat later the enemy again pounded Bolan and Yerzim's position with another relentless leadstorm.

Ducking behind the boulder with Yerzim right beside him, Bolan checked the sky and spotted the staggered line of gunships sweeping low over the gorge for a nap-of-the-earth attack. The gunmen around the transport truck suddenly ceased fire as walls of dust billowed down the gorge and the whine of rotor blades filled the air.

Bolan looked back as the Israeli chopper was swinging around, nose toward the attacking gunships, but it never got off a shot from its miniguns.

Three of the enemy aircraft unleashed a lightning barrage of rocket fire. Zigzag tails of flames seemed to mesh, knifing through the darkness, streaking on target as if the hellbombs were magnets drawn to the

Israeli chopper. Yerzim cursed as the helicopter was consumed a millisecond later by a tremendous ball of fire that screamed up the sides of the gorge, hurling twisted wreckage in every direction.

Out of the corner of his eye, Bolan caught the gunships, moving so fast and so low that they swept on, just feet over the climbing roar of the mushrooming fireball. He watched them surge past his position, recognizing the attack choppers as Mi-24 Hinds before they vanished beyond the eastern hills.

The Executioner returned grim attention to the battle. As fate would have it, Bolan saw a sheet of wreckage pound the earth just feet from the transport truck, showering sparks and hurling other pieces of flaming scrap over the enemy. It was enough to cause the gunmen to fear being crushed more than being killed by a bullet.

As they scrambled to pick themselves up, another flaming scrap dropped behind the gunners, illuminating them clearly in both Bolan and Yerzim's death sights. Sustained bursts from both men took down four of the enemy, their black uniforms holed by blistering lead. Bolan moved in, leapfrogging two boulders with catlike grace, Uzi poised to fire. Yerzim continued to pour it on, apparently venting his rage with clear overkill, scything through the enemy, sweeping his subgun swept back and forth until the clip ran dry.

Bodies all around were pitching to the hard-packed earth when Bolan spotted a gunman swing around the rear of the transport and unleash a chattering spray from his assault rifle. The warrior took cover behind a low, jagged wall of rock as he rammed a fresh clip into his Uzi. Yerzim loaded another 30-round magazine into his own weapon, then turned his attention to the lone survivor, quickly forcing the guy to retreat to the other side of the truck.

In the next moment, using the lull in enemy fire, Bolan rolled over the boulder, angled in for the truck, then nosedived to the ground. In the firelight the Executioner made out the lower half of a pair of legs on the other side of the truck. He cut loose with his Uzi, nearly amputating the guy's legs at the knees.

A hideous shriek knifed the air. Bolan was up and running, circling the front of the truck, sliding toward the passenger's side. Crouched, he looked around the side, found the guy on his back but swinging the assault rifle up and toward him. The enemy's face was a twisted mask of agony. Bolan put the gunman out of his misery with a 3-round burst to his chest.

Cautious, having had no time to take an enemy head count before the battle erupted, Bolan moved down the side of the truck. Working perfectly in tandem, as if Yerzim could read his mind, he met the Mossad agent at the back of the truck. He gave the Israeli a nod, brought up his Uzi, then threw the flap up but found nothing in the back of the transport.

"I'll drive," Yerzim said. "God only knows what we're going to find when we hit that compound."

"We'll be walking straight into hell—that's what we'll find," Bolan stated as he opened the passenger's door and hopped in.

THE FAINT SOUND OF ROTORS was music to Crocker's ears. The mercenary smiled. He didn't have to turn around to know what was coming in behind them. D day was in progress.

The soldier who had identified himself to the six of them as Sergeant Eitan was standing in the headlights of the Land Rover. Two other Galil-toting Israelis flanked Eitan. The soldiers looked confused and impatient. One of the men looked past Crocker, his expression tight with sudden alarm as the sound of rotors grew louder.

"Damn it, say something. I told you this is a secured area and you are to leave immediately," Eitan said.

When Crocker and the others didn't budge, the Israeli growled, "All right, get off those camels."

It was the last thing Sergeant Eitan ever said. Just as suddenly as the Israelis started to step away from the Land Rover, they froze at the sound of helicopters shrieking toward them from out of the darkness. Just as quickly Crocker and his strike team leaped off their camels, threw off their robes and unleashed their Uzis with relentless streams of death.

The three Israelis died with shock etched on their faces, six Uzis flaming and stitching them with sweeping bursts that lifted them off their feet and hurled them into the Land Rover. The camels, crying out in panic at the din of autofire, scattered in all directions. The headlights shattered under the hurricane of lead before the Uzis fell silent.

The gunships streaked over the carnage.

Dust sweeping over him, Crocker smiled grimly as he watched the Mi-24s sweep in low for the strafing run that would produce instant hell on earth.

SOMETHING HAD GONE WRONG. Even though Gorman didn't have time to waste pondering how the Israelis knew they were going to be attacked, he still couldn't help but wonder whether it was just a recon team sent out due to suspicion and paranoia on the part of the Israelis. Or had the Israeli's gotten to their man in place in the compound. Whatever, back at the gorge they had been forced to blow that Israeli chopper out of the sky.

Unfortunately Gorman had to leave Collins and his team behind to take care of the two soldiers Gorman had seen engaged in a firefight with his troops. They'd link up shortly. But the fact that the chopper with the Star of David was even there indicated that the Israelis suspected they were going to be attacked. Worse, the explosion and firefight in the gorge was close enough to the compound that if anyone was listening, the Israelis would have put the base on full alert. Gorman's Law was now going to be tested to the limit, he suspected as he stood behind the pilot and copilot.

The compound came into full view, everything growing rapidly before the bulletproof cockpit Plexiglas, the entire target area bathed in the white glow coming from the klieg lights: the American C-130; the huge fuel bin; Israeli choppers and ground vehicles; another grounded C-130 in the middle of the target area; soldiers all over the place, some scrambling, but most looking to Gorman like stick figures, frozen in shock and disbelief on the ground.

Over his headset Gorman bellowed, "Fire away, hit 'em with everything you've got!"

Gorman, an M-16 with an attached M-203 grenade launcher gripped tightly in his fists, a SPAS-12 slung across a shoulder, watched through the cockpit glass, adrenaline racing through his blood like wildfire, knowing this was the moment where they either won or lost it. Dozens of rockets streaked ahead, and the deafening roar of machine-gun fire from his gunships echoed through the open fuselage doorway.

Reuter stood behind Gorman, both men watching the sky fall on the compound with grim stares, almost laughing with morbid fascination.

Dead ahead Gorman saw the American C-130 erupt in a huge ball of fire, the behemoth aircraft blown apart in a series of titanic explosions that sent warped pieces of the hull razoring everywhere. The explosions and wreckage seemed to mesh as they swept up the bulk of the forces near the obliterated plane. Then Gorman felt his Mi-24 rock with the volcanic force of the eruption as they flew over the climbing fireclouds. Next he saw a line of explosions to the right and left flanks march over the compound, hurling dozens of those stick figures skyward.

The merc leader braced himself as the gunship went into a hairpin turn at the east end of the compound. In the next moment, as his helicopter began another strafing run over the compound, Gorman witnessed his worst fear come to life. In the far east and west corners of the compound, rockets streaked from the ground, and he cursed as two of his gunships became boiling fireballs.

"Take out those fireteams, east and west corners!" Gorman raged over his headset. "Condors Three and Four, I want my troops on the ground now! Somebody take out that fuel bin in the east corner! I want this whole fucking place on fire! I want a team dropped off at the southern end of the prison! Lion's Head is our top priority. Frag the door and go in! I want our principals and my people out of here in five minutes!"

"I got those bastards!" Rogers, Gorman's pilot, snarled, and unleashed a stream of rockets that obliterated the east rocket fireteam in a whooshing fireball.

IT HAD SOUNDED like distant thunder. All of them looked toward the C-130, scoured the desert beyond, then glanced at one another with what Colonel Yoraam thought was suspicion and alarm. No one said a word.

Colonel Yoraam was striding toward the prisoner holding area when that sound of thunder seemed to linger and echo in the desert. Warning bells started to sound in his head, telling him what he heard was the sound of an explosion in the distance. Then he consciously pushed his fear aside, wanting to believe that his suspicion and paranoia were undermining his judgment. It was best to round up the prisoners and turn them over to the Americans. Yoraam's mission in the desert was just about finished.

Yoraam was walking beside Colonel Marlin, followed by two dozen soldiers, half of them Israeli, half of them Green Berets. Three men flanked Marlin, grim-faced silent guys in black whom the American colonel hadn't introduced. Yoraam suspected they were CIA and he sensed that Marlin didn't care for them in the least. Marlin didn't look at them and didn't acknowledge their presence.

A moment later Yoraam noticed the American colonel giving his compound a scathing eye and saw him begin to scowl. Or was he making that face of pain again? Was he judging in a critical manner the layout, the openness of the compound? Still wondering what the hell was going on here? No radar, no radio, no antiaircraft batteries, just four teams with rocket launchers, everyone tense but the night offering nothing that anyone should be afraid of.

Yes, Yoraam was suspicious, but he couldn't confirm his suspicions, and the American colonel hadn't asked again if something was wrong here. Still, there was that haunted look—no, a look of rage buried deep in the colonel's eyes that made Yoraam wonder about Marlin. Both of them were older men, and both knew they were most likely given command over this mission out of respect by their respective countries when younger, maybe hungrier officers were probably saying behind their backs that the old men should be put out to pasture.

Yoraam and the Israeli-American contingent had just reached the prison's south face when he clearly heard the unmistakable chatter of autofire ring over the compound. And in that moment Yoraam knew he was right in suspecting they were going to be attacked, but feared it was too late. He caught Marlin's eye as the American colonel came alive with an alert and angry look. The two colonels whirled just as the gunships swooped for the C-130 and blew the aircraft off the runway in a series of volcanic fireballs that all but wiped out any nearby soldiers. In the few frozen moments of this grim reality, Yoraam could only watch as enemy gunships turned his compound into a sea of raging fire and flying shredded human beings.

Klieg lights were blown apart in balls of showering flames, stitching lines of machine-gun and rocket fire raking the entire compound. Yoraam couldn't believe his eyes. Soldiers were screaming and dying everywhere, chopped up by machine-gun fire or blown clear into the night sky on roaring balls of fire.

As the earth-shaking blasts marched toward them, Yoraam was forced to hit the ground and cover his head. The concussive blasts were so close the Israeli colonel couldn't hear anything for what seemed like an eternity. In fact, the world began to turn dark as his senses were pounded again and again by the close and tenacious blasts, the heat of scorching fire feeling like invisible claws tearing at his face.

The blasts seemed far away in the next moment, as they erupted, on and on, and a nauseous feeling welled in his stomach. Yoraam recognized the whoosh of shrapnel and debris, felt them rake his body, forcing him to stay planted, facedown in the dirt. Somehow he found the strength and resolve to look up and out over the compound just as two of the enemy gunships became roiling clouds of fire.

Then Yoraam witnessed the apocalyptic blow to any hopes of possibly defeating this sudden and shocking attack. A barrage of rocket fire blew the fuel bin. Waves of ignited fuel swept up dozens of ground troops, turning some of those soldiers into shrieking demons being burned alive. More explosions rocked the night from the direction of the fuel bin, and more soldiers were catapulted into the sky on screaming tongues of fire.

Suddenly Yoraam felt hands digging into his shoulders. A moment later he realized it was the American colonel who had hauled him upright. The man might have looked like a scarecrow, but he had the strength of Hercules. Colonel Marlin held an M-16, and his face streaked with blood. He scoured the compound with wild eyes, obviously hell-bent on becoming part of the action.

Stunned, Yoraam chanced a look behind. The night had become as bright as day, illuminated by the mountain of explosions to the east, bathing the living, the dead and the dying in a glowing white light. What struck Yoraam the most was all the dead American and Israeli soldiers strewed about like torn rag dolls. There was little left to do but try to survive.

Then Yoraam witnessed another incredible sight, but one that confirmed his worst suspicions.

Moving with grim purpose across the compound, Baumstein was cutting loose with his mini-Uzis. Yet he wasn't firing at the gunships or the enemy disembarking from those choppers. No, the traitor was mowing down scattered groups of Israelis, adding to the murderous chaos.

Yoraam snatched up a discarded Galil assault rifle. If he was going to die, he would see Agent Baumstein on his way to hell first.

COLONEL MARLIN SPOTTED the tall broad figure in the distance and froze. Firelight outlined the shape with the blazing M-16, and as the figure turned, the intense wavering glow from the sea of flames shone like a beacon on the hideous scar on that death's-head face. It was a face Marlin hadn't seen in years, but a face he would recognize anywhere.

Through the glaring wall of firelight, Marlin locked stares with the man he so desperately had wanted to kill all those years. Everything—the scattered but fierce firefights, the strafing gunships, the roaring balls of fire, the wreckage and bodies launched airborne on every point of the compass—was like some slow-motion movie sequence in the vision of Marlin's pulse-pounding sudden rage. At that moment nothing else seemed to matter to him.

With his young and very dead soldiers strewn in his wake, Marlin started to lift his M-16. Right away Gorman reacted to the threat, swinging his assault rifle around as another explosion thundered over the compound.

Neither Marlin nor Gorman got off a shot.

The colonel felt himself grabbed from behind and pulled to the ground. In the next instant he heard the brief stutter of weapons fire, a line of slugs belching puffs of dust beside him. A heartbeat later he looked up and saw a giant piece of flaming wreckage falling from the black sky. He covered his head as the wreckage hammered the earth just yards away, showering fire and sparks and dust in all directions.

When Marlin jumped to his feet, Gorman was a retreating shadow, sliding toward the north end of the prison. The colonel was about to go after the guy but autofire raked his position. Next thing Marlin knew, he was beating a fiery retreat across the compound, fighting for his life beside Yoraam and the three CIA agents as the enemy's fire pushed them toward the prison. Even as he retreated, firing at the distant shadows of Gorman and his men, Marlin was already searching for some way to get in close to his most hated enemy. It seemed impossible right then, but if he had to, Marlin would make a suicide charge if it looked as if Gorman was going to evacuate.

BOLAN TOOK IN the hellzone as the transport truck bore down on the battle. Even from a half mile away, he could see clearly the gunships had paved the way for potential enemy victory. Everything appeared destroyed and on fire. It was exactly what the Executioner had predicted.

Grim, Bolan looked at Yerzim. They were only two men, out in the middle of nowhere, cut off from the world, prepared to take on a greater enemy force that had seized the night by a shock attack. The Mossad man gripped the steering wheel so tight his knuckles were white. They both knew this was the worst-case nightmare scenario. They were about to move into a battle where they were taking their chances against not only enemy bullets, but by being mistaken for the enemy by their own people.

"If we draw fire from our own," Yerzim said, reading Bolan's look, "all I can do is try to tell them we're on their side."

Bolan, having no intention of firing on Americans or Israelis even to save his own skin, hoped that would be enough. The best way to take the fight to the enemy was to secure some sort of cover right away, pinpoint the enemy and take them out as they showed. There was so much confusion and terror in that compound, with what numbers were left of their side concentrating solely on killing the enemy or maybe just surviving at this point, Bolan knew they stood a good chance of joining the fight and not drawing fire from Israelis or Americans. At least not right away. If Bolan and Yerzim could notch an enemy body count as they linked up with what remained of their side, it should be proof enough of who they were to the surviving Israeli-American force.

As they closed on the flaming debris of the C-130, bodies and fiery or smoking wreckage scattered in all directions, Bolan picked out a spot where they could most likely close in on the enemy. He saw the bulk of the ground fighting was adjacent to a low-lying building on his left flank, and he suspected that structure was the prison holding Kamal.

Yerzim confirmed Bolan's suspicion. "That's the prison over there. They're taking it down!"

"Stop over there by the ground vehicles," Bolan told Yerzim, nodding at the line of vehicles dead ahead. "We'll take cover and close in from behind."

Yerzim grunted. The only possible cover left intact was indeed the Land Rovers, the Israeli choppers and the second C-130, which was grounded in the middle of the compound. Only moments earlier Bolan had seen the sky lit up by a volcanic eruption and knew the gunships had most likely blown the fuel bin to create even more chaos.

Bolan braced himself, Uzi in hand as the GAZ-66 broke the perimeter and Yerzim angled the vehicle toward the Land Rovers. The remaining Israeli and American soldiers were engaged in a firefight to the truck's far left flank, at the prison complex. Gunships continued to sweep over the compound, strafing the soldiers with flaming miniguns. Without any sort of cover, Bolan knew the soldiers were doomed.

He hopped out of the GAZ-66, the stench of burning gasoline and roasting flesh stinging his senses. Screams of agony knifed the air. A delayed explosion roared from somewhere on the compound, ringing Bolan's ears as he ran beside Yerzim for the shelter of the trucks. Then, as the two men secured cover behind the line of vehicles, Bolan knew they'd been spotted by one of the gunships.

A millisecond later the GAZ-66 was turned into flaming scrap by a tremendous fireball. Bolan saw the gunship hover directly over the middle of the compound, roughly two dozen yards away, then it began to spray the Land Rovers with a blazing storm of minigun fire. For long moments a hurricane of glass blew over Bolan and Yerzim, a stream of bullets whining off the ground behind them.

Bolan looked up through narrowed eyes and saw the gunship, still hovering, its miniguns suddenly and strangely silent, as if the pilot was either deciding what to do, had lost sight of his targets or was awaiting orders. Whichever, it gave Bolan precious seconds to look around for additional and heavier firepower. Behind him the Executioner spotted a discarded but armed RPG-7 near the battered body of an Israeli soldier.

6

Even as the Israelis viciously shoved them to the floor, shouting for all of them to be still and quiet, Aziz Kamal couldn't resist smiling. It was happening. The thunder of explosions beyond the walls of the prison, the screams of men in agony, the whine of rotor blades and the blister of machine-gun fire almost made him laugh.

But he wasn't free yet. He and his brothers in the holy war against the Jews and the Great Satan had just been chained together when the first of a seemingly endless series of explosions sounded from across the compound and rocked the prison. Gorman and his men had arrived, just as Baumstein had told him they would. Surely God, the compassionate and merciful, was on his side. Freedom was just minutes away.

Kamal looked up and saw the panic and confusion on the faces of the Israeli soldiers. He knew Gorman, and he was certain the soldiers were doomed. For the Israelis there was only death.

The Iraqi kept craning his neck, searching for the soldier who had the keys to his chains. He saw the man striding for the far door at the end of the cell block, heard that soldier barking orders for his men to cover the prisoners. The door suddenly exploded in his face. Dust and debris blew down the cell block on a screaming ball of fire, forcing Kamal to hug the floor. Then he heard the merciless chatter of autofire and looked back to see Israelis dropping to the ground, their uniforms chopped into bloody rags.

As the flaming muzzles of automatic weapons ceased firing and some of the dust cleared, Kamal recognized one of the freedom fighters as the Briton, Miller. He and a half dozen of Gorman's finest burst through the opening, their weapons blazing again. The few Israelis who had survived the grenade blast were dispatched within moments. But another group of soldiers stood at the other end of the corridor.

Kamal saw them whirl toward Miller, prepared to fire, when a grenade blast erupted within feet of their position. The Iraqi watched with grim anticipation and burning anxiety. It was strange, he thought, that it had all happened so fast, but it felt like an eternity.

The first grenade explosion at the north end of the corridor had been meant to blow the door in; the second blast was intended to take out the soldiers grouped there. Survivors began scrabbling for discarded weapons, coughing, staggering to their feet. Then, through the churning dust and cordite, Kamal instantly recognized a pair of burning eyes that looked as if they belonged more to the devil than a human.

As wounded Israelis kept groaning and struggling to stand, Gorman rolled through the jagged hole in the wall, then parted the dust with his SPAS-12 thundering away with flaming bursts of instant and gory death. It was a beautiful sight to Kamal as the big merc calmly fired his automatic shotgun, point-blank, into Israelis. The roaring blasts kicked two soldiers off their feet, nearly cutting them in two.

When the last Israeli soldier in the corridor had been taken down by Gorman, Kamal shouted, "The keys! At the other end!"

Gorman nodded at Reuter, who ran past the line of outstretched prisoners. A moment later Kamal found himself looking up at his savior, who grinned down at him as if he didn't have a care in the world. Gorman, Kamal decided, was indeed a devil in human skin. The man was insane.

"How ya doin', Aziz? You ready to do some business?"

Kamal marveled at the man's ice-cold acceptance of all the murder and mayhem, as he himself was starting to feel some panic. "Just get these chains off us and get us out of here!"

"I'll take that response as affirmative, mister."

The smile on Gorman's face vanished as the radio handset on the mercenary leader's webbing crackled.

"Condor One to Lion's Head, come in."

"Yeah," Gorman barked into his radio handset.

"We've got a problem, Major. We've neutralized most of the ground forces, but those two we saw back at the wadi just arrived in our transport truck. I neutralized the truck, but it looks like they've secured cover. I lost sight of them."

Kamal spotted a flicker of confusion and fear in Gorman's eyes.

"I don't give a damn what you have to do, but take them out. Radio Tripps first. We're evacuating now!" Gorman growled. "You got that?"

"Roger."

Gorman held the radio handset by his side and shouted to his troops at the north end. "Cover the door. We're out of here!"

Kamal stood as Reuter began unlocking the chains. The radio crackled again.

"Tripps is on the way, sir," the pilot stated. Then, a second later, he screamed, "He's got an RPG!"

Gorman froze, a look of disbelief on his face.

"He's locking on to us, goddamn it!" the copilot screamed.

Kamal found himself staring into Gorman's burning eyes as the mercenary leader listened intently. There was the sound of machine-gun fire over the handset, then a tremendous explosion, followed by utter silence.

No one said anything. The mercenaries and the Iraqi terrorists all looked expectantly at Gorman, but before he could respond, two of Gorman's men toppled through the blown opening at the north end, their chests riddled with bloody holes. Kamal dived to the floor as gunfire erupted from behind him and bullets pounded the interior of the cells and the ceiling.

BOLAN LIFTED the RPG-7. As Yerzim fired on the group of enemy soldiers who had secured the north side of the prison, the Executioner sighted on the Mi-24, triggering the 40 mm warhead just as the gunship's miniguns began to cut loose again. The tracking line of slugs danced past Bolan, who had flung himself against the side of a Land Rover.

The warhead streaked toward the helicopter and detonated on impact, the force of the explosion spewing wreckage in all directions.

Bolan cast the spent rocket launcher aside. As the fiery remains of the obliterated gunship rained to the ground, the Executioner saw a group of five black-garbed figures break from the prison. They either had orders from Gorman to seek out Bolan and Yerzim, or they were acting on their own. Whichever it was, the hardmen opened fire with assault rifles, fanning out.

With autofire peppering the Land Rovers, Bolan and Yerzim sought cover behind the last vehicle. Another gunship hovered in the area, pouring a steady stream of fire at the Land Rovers. As tires blew and glass exploded, the two men dived to the ground. A quick look into the compound moments later revealed to Bolan that the gunship had swung around and was streaking toward the prison.

The Executioner stood and moved forward in a crouch, grimly intent on taking the fight to the advancing enemy. But yet another gunship entered the fray, sweeping over the C-130 ruins, then landing at the prison's north end. As enemy bullets peppered their cover, Bolan was forced to put the firefight at the prison out of his mind.

GORMAN SAW FOUR of his men go down during the initial attack from the south end of the corridor. He had forgotten all about Marlin and the Israeli colonel, believing Miller and his team would have eliminated that threat before initiating their part of the assault.

Evacuation wasn't guaranteed. They were in danger of being trapped in the prison corridor, or worse, like his downed gunships, blown out of the sky when they lifted off. Gorman didn't have time to think about casualties. He was concerned only with getting out of there with his principals.

The merc leader fired his M-16 at Marlin, the Israeli colonel and the three men in black who were triggering pistols. It had been the wall of flesh of his own men, Gorman saw, that had saved his own life. Sarjir, two of the ex-CIA operatives and a few of his other fighters were now motionless in pools of blood.

"Move it out! Move, move!" Gorman bellowed. Through the dust and the cordite, he saw the raw hatred and savage determination on the face of Marlin, who stood at the far end of the corridor, and opened fire.

The two men locked eyes, and Gorman felt frozen for a long moment in a time warp of bad memories. Yesterday's trials had become today's obstacles. The guy whose family he had killed in Vietnam, the soldier he had believed he had killed in Cambodia, wanted him dead.

Retreating, Gorman poured it on with his M-16, firing past Reuter and Miller, the ex-SAS commando and South African soldier covering the evac from the corridor with tenacious twin streams of lead. Gorman saw Marlin and his team whirl around the corner of the hole in the southern end. Suddenly one of the guys in black was dancing a jig of death as a line of slugs from the barking assault rifles marched up his chest, flinging him beyond the doorway.

With the sound of crackling flames and the din of autofire in his ears, Gorman moved outside. As he backed toward the gunship's open fuselage doorway, he searched the entire compound. Just about everything had been destroyed. Dead men were strewed in torn and twisted heaps everywhere, both his and the enemy's. Still, there was so much black smoke wafting across the compound that it was difficult for Gorman to make out anyone who might be advancing on them from out there. But the firestorm clearly outlined the immediate vicinity around his evac chopper, and nothing appeared to be moving.

He had enjoyed about as complete a success as he had hoped for. But were the two soldiers who had brought down one of his choppers and had apparently eliminated Collins and his team in the wadi still out there? It didn't matter, Gorman decided, knowing they had to get out of there if he wanted to collect on a twenty-million-dollar payday.

Gorman grabbed his radio handset, cursing the fact that he had only three attack choppers left. Those choppers were now grounded by the prison face, the pilots awaiting further orders. He saw the Israeli C-130 and choppers were still intact and knew what had to be done in order to cover the evacuation and hopefully take out the rest of the enemy.

Then Gorman spotted Baumstein running toward him through the swirling dust. The merc leader had the urge to kill the Israeli right there, but good judgment told him to interrogate the man to find out just what had gone wrong.

"Get the fuck in the chopper!" Gorman roared at Baumstein.

Teeth gritted, Gorman shoved two Iraqis, who were taking in the carnage with a grim eye of approval, into the Mi-6. "Get your asses in the chopper!"

Then he raised his radio handset to give his pilots the final order as their principals scrambled aboard the evac chopper. A moment later autofire sparked off the hull of the Mi-6. Gorman flinched as slugs grazed his face, then saw two of the Iraqis tumble to the dirt, their blood spraying through the air. Once again, as fate would have it, someone else had bought a bullet for him. Gorman chuckled.

BOLAN'S SUBGUN CHURNED out a relentless stream of 9 mm slugs. Still crouched by the flaming hull of the downed gunship, he knew the unarmed shadows fleeing the prison and attempting to board the evac chopper were Kamal and his terrorist brothers.

Together with Yerzim, Bolan managed to cut down more than a half dozen of the terrorists, all of whom he knew were hungry for freedom so they could again kill innocents. He saw the surviving escapees pick up the pace in blind panic, some of them trampling their own wounded to secure cover in the gunship's hull.

Three of the gunships lifted off. Even though their position was blanketed by drifting sheets of thick black smoke, making it difficult for the enemy to pinpoint their exact position, Bolan knew even a wildly placed salvo of rocket fire would rip them to pieces.

The gunships swung around and began pounding out a barrage of rockets. Fireballs erupted around the compound, churning up the earth, scattering flaming debris in all directions.

The concussive blast of a nearby explosion knocked Bolan and Yerzim to the ground. Not wasting a precious second, the Executioner was up and running, yanking the Israeli to his feet. Out of the corner of his eye, he saw the C-130 in the middle of the compound go up in flames. Strafing rounds from the miniguns drilled into the Israeli choppers. Bolan, sprinting for the deepest corner of the compound, looked over his shoulder.

The Mi-24 gunships pounded the prison with more rocket fire, giant slabs of rubble hurling into the sky. The entire compound became a blinding white light of massive explosions. A line of minigun fire suddenly swept over the Land Rovers, Bolan and Yerzim sprinting in a zigzag as several of the vehicles were turned into roiling balls of fiery scrap. It seemed as if the gunships were unleashing everything they had left.

Bolan kept pumping his legs, straining to reach cover. But it wasn't enough. In the next instant, as he began to dive over a scrap of wreckage, Bolan felt himself propelled by one final ear-shattering, earth-shaking explosion. He was aware of being airborne, felt the heat of the blast clawing at his backside.

When the Executioner hit the earth, he saw a supernova of white light explode in his sight. Then everything went black.

GORMAN STOOD in the doorway of the Mi-6. The compound and its perimeter were engulfed in fire, just as he had planned. It was a fearsome sight to behold. Even as his gunships quickly put distance to the killing field, the firestorm burned bright and fierce, lighting the desert world for hundreds of yards in every direction. With the sea of flames and the roiling clouds of black smoke consuming every inch of the compound, it was impossible to tell if anyone was moving among the carnage. Gorman was mesmerized by the sight. Phase one had been a costly success—costly, that was, for any of his men who had died there.

As he heard the groans and the cries of pain behind him, Gorman put his mind on the next step. Turning, he saw Kamal holding one of the Iraqis in his arms.

"Youssef, hold on, you will make it, my brother," Kamal told the man.

He'd been gut shot, and Gorman knew he was dying quickly. The guy was bleeding all over the floor of the chopper, holding in his guts, and Kamal was coddling the guy like some newborn infant with measles. Gorman felt a mounting anger. It was a disgusting sight.

Kamal looked up at the big American. "We need to get him help."

Gorman looked away and saw Baumstein sitting in the shadows of the gunship. As the merc leader walked toward the cockpit, he said, "I'll deal with you shortly. Give you time to think up some line of bullshit."

He joined the pilot and copilot. "I want a head count of my men. Get me a list of names. Stay on course for our base. We'll refuel there, then we'll fly into Jordan. Our antiradar shields still operative?"

As his pilots gave him an affirmative, Gorman took a step down the fuselage. He suspected his casualties were severe. First guesstimate was that his force had been cut by half. Hammersmith, Judd, Reuter and Miller were the only ones in the gunship he could count on. There were the ex-CIA assassins, eight others in his force, and maybe twenty-five Iraqis gathered in the evac chopper. Gorman hadn't seen any sign of Collins and Crocker. He knew he'd left behind seriously wounded, but everyone had known the deal going in. It wasn't as if he called the shots from the safety of a command post far away from the battle. So he wasn't about to listen to any squawking about wounded being left where they fell.

"You must help him!" Kamal pleaded.

Gorman didn't have time for that. Without hesitation, he walked up to the dying Iraqi, drew his .45 and pumped three rounds into the man's chest. The body thudded to the floor.

Kamal was stunned as he stared at the blood on his hands. The other Iraqis looked at Gorman in fear and horror.

As he lowered the .45 to his side, Gorman pinned Kamal with an icy look. "You ready to give praise to the real Allah and talk business now?"

7

Bolan was aware of someone shaking him, then heard, "Mr. Belasko? Mr. Belasko?"

Yerzim's voice seemed to reach Bolan from miles away. For what seemed like an eternity, he saw nothing but total blackness and felt unable to move. Then slowly pain began to knife through every nerve ending, finally pulling his being into one central core of fire. At least he knew he was alive. The last thing he could remember was the shockingly loud rush of fireballs, launched on the pounding force of the blasts, hammering the ground on his head.

"This him? The Justice guy, Belasko? Hell, he doesn't look so tough now, does he? He alive?"

The second voice was cold and edged with anger and a hint of suspicion. Maybe contempt.

"Yes, he's alive. If I didn't know better, I would think you're disappointed."

"A lot of Americans died here, pal. I'm hardly disappointed."

"Do not forget, sir, that an awful lot of Israelis died here also."

Somehow Bolan pried his eyes open. Light speared in, forcing him to retreat into darkness. When he opened his eyes again, he coughed for a long moment as his senses were assaulted by the pungent smoke. While he lay there on his back, the world a fractured haze of bright and burning light, he moved an arm, stifling a groan, then tried his legs. Nothing was broken. Lady luck had chosen to smile on him.

"Easy, Mr. Belasko. Here, let me help you stand."

"That's okay," Bolan said, dredged up the strength and stood. His legs were rubbery, the world spinning in his eyes for long moments before slowly coming to a stop.

As his vision cleared, Bolan saw the first rays of dawn had broken over the Sinai. The carnage Bolan saw was mind-boggling. Gorman had succeeded. There was nothing left but smoke, fire and death everywhere.

Bolan flexed his hands, then rolled his head to shake out the cobwebs.

"Look, I don't know what business this is of the Justice Department, pal, but I've got a huge problem on my hands. I sincerely hope you won't become part of it."

Bolan's gaze narrowed as he stared at the sharp face and the angry eyes burning back at him.

"Uh, this is Crueller," Yerzim told Bolan. "He's apparently CIA."

"CIA? You come here to clean up a mess or start a new one?"

Crueller tensed and gritted his teeth, looking as if he wanted to take a swing at him. Bolan waited, but the guy didn't make a move or say anything. Then the Executioner looked at Yerzim. The Mossad man had taken some cuts and abrasions to his face during that last series of explosions. Blood and soot covered the man's grim visage.

"I was knocked unconscious myself, Mr. Belasko," Yerzim said. "We were both very fortunate. I have to believe those gunships expended every last round."

"How many survivors?" Bolan asked.

"With the exception of another CIA man, who is checking to see if any of the choppers are operational, that's it," Yerzim said, then nodded past Bolan.

Bolan turned, looking in the direction Yerzim indicated. Two men stood at the far eastern end of the runway, beyond the smoldering, twisted heaps of wreckage. He recognized the uniforms and respective berets of the IDF and U.S. Special Forces. A dozen bodies were stretched out beside the two men. The wounded had been covered in blankets, some of the soldiers hooked up to IV bottles.

"Colonel Yoraam of the IDF and Colonel Marlin of Special Forces," Yerzim informed Bolan.

The Executioner heard the distinctive and familiar sound of a death rattle and watched as the Israeli colonel pulled a blanket over the face of a soldier.

"And a handful of seriously wounded," Yerzim went on. "I doubt that any of them will make it. We are not fully equipped to treat this many casualties."

"Doesn't seem like you were equipped for much more, either," Crueller growled. "How the hell was it you people didn't know about this attack? How the hell could an armada of Russian attack helicopters slip through your radar and blow this compound up so badly it looks like the day after the Apocalypse? A full-frontal air assault, and not a damn thing here that looks like an antiaircraft battery. Un-fucking-believable. I think it's time you stepped aside and let the CIA take charge from here on out."

"I believe the CIA did take charge here, Crueller," Bolan said. "One of your former employees is responsible for what you see. My question to you would be if this Gorman is such a terror and such a thorn in the CIA's side, how was it that you forgot about him all these years until now?"

Crueller stiffened with anger. "I can tell already you and me are going to have a problem, Mr. Justice."

Bolan put some steel into his eyes and voice. "Trust me. There won't be any problem between us."

He ignored the CIA agent's scowl and headed toward the two colonels, Yerzim on his heels.

"He has a point, I'm afraid," Yerzim stated. "Unfortunately what this attack tells us is that Gorman's resources are far and wide. Perhaps he got help from the Syrians or the Jordanians. Obviously he was allowed to fly through their airspace unmolested."

"It could be the Jordanians and Syrians are helping him, but I doubt it. I think he either just got lucky, or he's stone-cold insane. He'll take out anything and anybody who gets in his way. It doesn't matter if they're Jordanians, Syrians or anybody else."

"I believe you are right, Mr. Belasko. This Gorman is obviously very much insane—to the point where he is willing to commit suicide to achieve whatever his aim is. Be that as it may, this was a well-planned and well-financed assault. If it turns out Syria or any extreme fundamentalist factions in Jordan that are unhappy with the new peace accord between our countries helped him, this entire mess could have devastating results. You can forget about any lasting peace in this part of the world."

"Nothing's changed," Bolan said. "Kamal and his people are free. Gorman is out there. Our people are all but wiped out here."

"Meaning you intend to go after Gorman."

"Yeah, I do."

"If you go after Gorman, I must insist that I come along. It has now become personal. Baumstein, I believe, escaped with Gorman."

"Unless he's shot down by Israeli F-16s, Gorman's going to disappear, probably into Syria, maybe Iraq. I think your boy, Kaballah, knows more than he's telling us. May I make a suggestion?"

"You want to talk to Kaballah again."

"Right. But I've also got a plan that could help lead us right to Gorman. I'll tell you about it later."

Bolan came face-to-face with the two colonels. Both Yoraam and Marlin looked angry enough to kill someone with their bare hands. Yoraam pulled the blanket over yet another soldier who breathed his last.

"You must be Mr. Belasko of the Justice Department," Colonel Marlin stated.

At first Bolan was a little surprised. Marlin looked incredibly frail, withered almost to a human shell, as if he might be suffering from some terminal illness. But Bolan focused on the determination and strength in the man's eyes, the kind of strength born from the endurance of suffering, of seeing and knowing the horrors that the world could inflict.

"Yes, sir, that's right."

"I understand from Agent Yerzim that the two of you inflicted some serious casualties on our opposition before Gorman nearly blew you two out of existence. You can see for yourself your help wasn't enough, but I'll welcome any extra guns with me." The colonel paused, and Bolan read his message of vengeance loud and clear. "Mr. Belasko, I'm not sure you know exactly what is going on here...."

"I know enough," Bolan said, a flicker of compassion showing in his eyes as he gazed into the colonel's face. "I was briefed about you and Gorman."

"Then you know how badly I want this bastard."

"Just as badly as I want the son of a bitch who helped them," Colonel Yoraam said, shutting the eyelids on one of his dead troops, then standing and staring at Bolan and Yerzim.

Suddenly Bolan heard one of the choppers' rotors whir to life. Pivoting, he found Crueller walking toward them.

"Two other choppers are still intact," the agent barked. "You've got full fuel tanks in both. I'm out of here. You people are on your own."

"It would look like we've always been on our own," Marlin snarled.

"What was that, Colonel?"

Marlin laid a sharp stare on the CIA man. "I said I've been on my own for twenty years. What's so different now?"

"Look, you people, this is CIA business from here on. If you're thinking about going after Gorman, forget it. What you need to do is get your wounded back to Israel. I'll contact my people in Israel, do some damage control. What I'm going to do is try and keep what happened here out of the world's headlines as long as possible. Go home."

"Just like that, you're going to take off after him," Marlin growled.

"That's right, just like that. I've got a special task force on standby. You already knew my mission, Colonel. I was supposed to interrogate Kamal and find out where the rest of his people were, then go after them. Because of this entirely fucked-up mess here, it looks like my game plan's been altered a little. Do the smart thing, people, and stay out of my way."

Crueller ran a hard gaze over the four men, then wheeled and headed for his chopper. Bolan watched, feeling the tension mount among the group. He suspected how the rest of them wanted to proceed.

As the helicopter lifted off, Yoraam told the group, "Help me get our wounded into one of those choppers. We can talk on the way back to Israel."

THEY AGREED ON ONE THING—Gorman, Kamal and the others had to be hunted down, and the four of them had to be the ones who did it. The problem was how to go about doing that.

Bolan stood near the cockpit as Yerzim guided the chopper over the Sinai Desert, the wasteland beyond the cockpit window now bathed in the first full rays of morning sunlight. In grim silence Bolan watched as Yoraam and Marlin checked their wounded. It had been a complete disaster for the Israeli-American force. For now the dead had to be left behind, and the two colonels could only make the wounded as comfortable as possible. And hope for the best.

The hunt for Gorman had to get underway immediately. Every second that passed meant the enemy was getting that much farther away. They had to go after Gorman and the others soon after they touched down in Israel to unload the wounded, but there could be complications with the Israeli and American governments. He just hoped international red tape didn't hinder them. Everyone would now want a piece of Gorman. Politicians would want answers, Bolan knew, and there would be people screaming for heads to roll over this fiasco. Yoraam and Marlin were the likely scapegoats, but if they were worried about the fallout or their futures, they hadn't said a word regarding either.

What had happened at the prison compound was only the beginning. The worst, Bolan suspected, was yet to come. The mission had now, indeed, become intensely personal. He clearly read the hunger for vengeance in the eyes of the two colonels. At least they all had the same objective. But with Marlin, there was more than twenty years of hate stored up for Gorman, itching for release. Hate was dangerous. It could blind a man to all reason, especially when a man's family had been murdered and the scent of that murderer's blood was in his nose. Bolan understood that all too well. He didn't have any problem with the colonel wanting his revenge, but he decided he'd have to be careful when they collided with Gorman again. And one way or another, Bolan knew they'd find

Gorman. None of them would be able to rest until they did.

Yoraam addressed Bolan. "The only way my country will sanction us to go after Gorman and the others is for me to assemble a commando unit."

"Okay," Bolan said. "How quickly could you have that done?"

"Within an hour after we land."

"I can have the proper authorities contacted in Jordan to let them know what has happened and what we're doing," Yerzim told the group. "I'll handle getting us passports and identification. I don't see any problem with us being able to move freely through Jordan. But if Gorman and Kamal slip into Syria, or worse, Iraq, that would be a major obstacle. If that happens, we would be completely on our own."

"You understand," Yoraam told Bolan, "that the families of the casualties from both our countries have to be informed. I can only keep what happened back there from becoming public knowledge for only so long. A day, two at the most."

"That'll give us enough time to at least pick up their trail," Bolan said.

"It better. The U.S. Embassy in Israel will have to be informed of American casualties," Marlin said. "This whole mess is going to have international repercussions. I don't so much care about what the world thinks. I don't even care at this point how much of my ass gets chewed off when word of this gets out.

I just don't want us hindered in any way from going after Gorman."

There was grim conviction in Yerzim's voice as he said, "There will not be any hindrance. I assure you."

"My country will want to send in their own, uh, hunting expedition," Marlin said. "But by the time they've assembled a force and flown them here, I damn well intend to have Gorman's head in my hand. And I intend to get to Gorman before those CIA clowns do."

"I think we need to address another potential problem," Bolan told the group. "The Russians."

"What about the Russians?" Marlin asked.

Bolan told the colonels about Kaballah and what the Iraqi had related about the arms deal.

"So, you think the Russians may send people after Gorman, too?" Yoraam said.

Bolan nodded. "It's possible, if they're not looking for him already. I can't see the Russians sitting around doing nothing."

"The fact that this soured arms deal between Gorman and rogue Russian agents has been kept quite leads me to believe that the Russians will do something about it," Yerzim stated.

"We'll deal with the Russians if and when we cross their paths," Bolan said.

A wounded soldier suddenly groaned. Marlin went to the young Special Forces soldier and took his hand.

"Easy, son, take it easy. Just hold on. We're going to get you help."

Yerzim turned and addressed Bolan. "You want to tell me now how it is you intend to pick up Gorman's trail?"

"We're going to turn Kaballah loose," Bolan answered.

Yerzim stared at Bolan as if he were crazy.

THEY HAD REFUELED and were now deep into Jordanian airspace. Gorman checked the rugged desert terrain. Nothing but sand and rock for as far as the eye could see. If they stayed away from major Jordanian cities and towns, they should have no problem reaching the Syrian border. If they were stopped by Jordanian authorities, Gorman would handle them one of two ways: with a cash contribution or blazing lead. He wasn't about to stop until he had the twenty million in hand and was safely on his way to Southeast Asia. So far, so good.

Gorman decided it was time to deal with Baumstein. He walked over to the Mossad man and pinned him with an icy stare. He felt the eyes of Kamal and his own men boring into the back of his head. With Baumstein clearly on the hot seat, Gorman let the silence drag. He watched the guy sweat for a few moments, then told him, "I don't see where you're going to do me any good from here on."

"We had a deal."

The merc leader almost laughed at the guy's boldness and hoped he would go for those mini-Uzis so he could finish him off with a couple of rounds from his .45. He was just about to tell the Mossad man that deals were made to be broken, when he caught himself, thinking ahead. Just maybe Baumstein could be used down the road. The guy was a traitor, and the Israelis would want him back. If nothing else, Gorman could use Baumstein as a hostage, a bargaining chip in the event the Israelis somehow caught up to them. Besides, it would look better to Kamal if he dealt straight with Baumstein, a show of good intent.

"What the hell, huh?" Gorman said, softening his tone. "Okay. We had a deal. Problem is, you're going to have to ride this out with us until I get paid."

"Do I have any choice?" Baumstein asked.

"None of us has a choice," Gorman replied. "That's both the beauty and the horror of it."

Gorman turned his attention to Kamal. The Iraqi didn't look happy. After shooting the wounded man, Gorman had tossed him off the gunship from a thousand feet up. If there was vengeance or hatred in Kamal's heart toward him, Gorman would find out soon enough. The slightly cold look Kamal gave the merc leader was enough to warn him to be careful of the Iraqi and his brothers in terror. They weren't about to forgive him so easily.

"Until you can get into Iraq and make it back with my money, where's the safest place we can hold out?" Gorman asked.

"The place where we originally negotiated the deal," Kamal said. "al-Shuraq."

Gorman smiled. "Exact same place I had in mind. Perfect. Close enough to the Iraqi border and close enough to where I stashed the merchandise. Only problem is, you'll be home among your brothers in this town. You've got what, maybe fifty brothers in Hamas and other groups holed up in al-Shuraq, armed to the teeth?"

"What are you saying?"

"I'm saying I don't want any surprises, Aziz. I want my twenty million in cash. Just like we talked about before you went and got yourself caught in Gaza."

"You are asking for quite a lot of money."

"The Russians wanted thirty million. I'm cutting you a sweet deal. Let's not squabble over a few million. I know you've got contacts inside Iraq—hell, you know Saddam personally. That guy still has access to huge amounts of cash, all the oil money I'm sure he plundered and is saving for a rainy day. Well, it's raining now. You tell him I've got the kind of firepower that can make him more than just some dangerous clown. If he doesn't want it, I'll take it somewhere else."

"Speaking of this twenty-million-dollar merchandise," Aziz said, his gaze narrowing, "do you think it would be too much trouble to let me see it first?"

Okay, the guy didn't trust him. Gorman knew right then how it was all going to play. He put on an easy smile. "No problem, Aziz."

BOLEN, AGENT WEISSKOPF, Yerzim and Colonel Marlin had gathered at the Israeli-Jordanian border. All of them were watching Kaballah, who was looking at the four-wheel-drive jeep with confusion.

Bolan waited, sweating a little under the blaze of the late-morning sun. Time was wasting, and he wanted to get on with the hunt. But Kaballah was looking the vehicle over as if he expected it to blow up in his face. The jeep was rigged, all right, but not with dynamite or plastique. Just before they had landed by helicopter on the border, a Mossad agent had planted a homing device in the vehicle. Bolan had the backup homing device on him.

"The keys are in it," Yerzim said. "There's plenty of gas and water to get you far away from here."

"Get going before I change my mind," Weisskopf told the Iraqi.

The confusion in Kaballah's eyes changed to suspicion. The Iraqi looked past the foursome, staring at the Arab village just beyond the low-lying hills, a half mile or so west.

Weisskopf glanced over her shoulder at the village, then told the man, "There's nothing and no one there, or in any part of this country for you. Ever again. Should you return here, I will hunt you down and kill you."

Kaballah chuckled. "You think I am stupid? I know why you are setting—"

"Do not say another word, Kaballah!" Yerzim snarled. "Get in and leave, or I will shoot you dead right here and right now myself."

"One last thing," Bolan said, stepping up to the Iraqi, who tensed with fear. "I think this is the least I owe you."

Bolan cracked a right off the Iraqi's jaw that dropped Kaballah on his back. He toed the Iraqi and saw he was out cold. None of the others had reacted to the sudden attack. They had already discussed this part of the plan. Bolan attached the small, flat homing device to the inside of Kaballah's belt. If the Iraqi ditched the jeep, the homing device on his belt had a two-hundred-mile range.

The Executioner looked beyond the Arab village, listening for the whir of rotor blades that would tell him Yoraam was landing with his commando unit.

"How long?" Bolan asked Yerzim.

"We'll wait in the village," the agent replied as the group began walking together. "The colonel should arrive within thirty minutes."

"Good. That will give us time to iron out some final details."

A few moments later Bolan heard Kaballah groan. He turned and saw the Iraqi stagger to his feet, rubbing his jaw. The terrorist wasted no more time. He hopped in the Jeep and in the next few moments was moving quickly across the Jordanian wasteland.

"There goes our pigeon," Yerzim said, tight-lipped. "One, we hope, that will lead us right to his master."

8

As soon as they set foot in the narrow dirt streets of al-Shuraq, two things became quickly apparent to Gorman. First Kamal was greeted by a small army of his Islamic brothers as if he were a conquering hero returning home. Second the Islamic extremists were all toting AK-47s or RPG rocket launchers. The first thing was an annoying spectacle. The second matter put Gorman on alert, since he was down to twenty-six men.

At first head count, he figured the terrorists hiding in al-Shuraq numbered forty, maybe fifty strong. Yet more could be inside the countless yellow stone dwellings that made up the town at the very edge of northeast Jordan. Put them together with Kamal's two dozen thugs...well, Gorman knew he could have a serious problem on his hands. Top it all off with the fact that Kamal could still be angry about his blowing away his wounded buddy and dumping him off his gunship. All hell could break loose any time. But Gorman was stuck. Unfortunately, at least for the moment, he needed Kamal, who had the necessary contacts inside Iraq to land him the deal of a lifetime.

It got worse, but in another way. What Gorman had neglected to tell his own men was that he couldn't pay them until the deal was nailed down and he had the twenty million in hand. Kamal, Gorman knew, could get the money—not, he *would* get the money, or the Iraqi was going to suffer a fate worse than anything he would have experienced had he been extradited to the U.S.

Gorman had done enough clandestine work for the CIA and had worked for and against enough terrorist groups to know that major terrorists had access to huge amounts of money or they wouldn't be able to operate freely and successfully. It was now just a question of convincing Kamal to do straight business, then getting the Iraqi to put his hands on that money. And Saddam had the money. Before the Gulf War, oil accounted for more than one-third of the Iraqi gross domestic product.

Gorman knew the economic data, but better yet he knew the real deal, and the real deal was knowing human nature, finding its weaknesses and exploiting them. Before Saddam's disaster at Kuwait, the Iraqis were pumping out almost two million barrels per day, their oil revenue estimated at nearly twelve billion U.S. dollars a year. It was criminal but believable that Saddam had siphoned off a whole lot of U.S. dollars during the fat years to either fund his war machine or build a cash reserve for himself, or both. That, Gorman had seen repeatedly, was the method to a tyrant's madness. Go for broke, kick some ass, but if it all started to crumble, make sure you could get away with what you had plundered from the people you claimed to support and defend. It all boiled down to greed.

Feeling the situation in al-Shuraq could blow up in his face, Gorman gave Reuter and Miller a quick look that silently told them to be alert and on guard.

Trailing Kamal down a narrow street that was choked with goats, camels, Japanese pickup trucks and half-naked kids, Gorman kept his guard up. If nothing else he was a realist, and that meant trusting no one on the other side. Despite the fact he and his men had freed Kamal, they were still unknown and distrusted factors on enemy turf, fifty miles from the Iraqi border and twenty miles from the Syrian border, outnumbered and outgunned in an armed haven for Islamic fanatics.

Gorman watched with a mix of anxiety and some contempt as Kamal was swarmed by an ever-growing number of Islamic rebels. They clapped one another on the shoulders, hugged, kissed cheeks, laughed. You'd think the guy was the Second Coming, Gorman thought, trying to hide what he felt since Kamal's associates were looking at the mercenaries with some suspicion. Okay, they were the infidels, tools of the Great Satan. Gorman could live with that. What he couldn't stomach much longer was that bittersweet stink of dung, tobacco smoke and spice cloying his noise. Al-Shuraq smelled like an open sewer.

Grimly aware of potential trouble, Gorman's men fanned out, taking both sides of the street. The merc leader looked his men over, trying to appear as indifferent as possible until he noticed Baumstein was hanging back the most, looking as if he were trying to decide something. Gorman threw the Mossad man a quick, menacing glare, then turned his grim attention back to the wildly cheering throngs. From down the street, near some market stalls, more Arab men in *kaffiyehs* were running to greet Kamal.

Gorman glanced at Miller and couldn't resist grumbling to the Briton, "Spare me, I know."

"What are we, chopped liver?" Miller muttered.

Suddenly the crowd of Arabs around Kamal parted. A moment later Gorman spotted a slightly built man in a red-and-white-checkered *kaffiyeh,* an AK-47 slung across his shoulder, striding toward Kamal. The Arab's eyes were wide in disbelief.

"Abdullah," Kamal said in greeting.

"Aziz. Is it really you, or do my old eyes deceive me?"

Gorman watched with mounting irritation as the two Arabs embraced, kissed each other on the cheeks, then stared with beaming eyes at each other.

"You are free? How?" Abdullah said, his face still frozen in disbelief. Then, as he noticed Gorman and his men, the crowd on the street suddenly became very still and quiet. Gorman found himself looking at a sea of suspicious and hostile faces.

Only the bleat of goats and sheep broke the tight silence. Gorman tensed as Kamal looked at him over his shoulder.

"Do you remember this man?" Kamal asked. "Major Gorman?"

"The one you said killed the Russians? Yes, I remember him," Abdullah replied, the Arab's tone of voice leaving Gorman more uncertain and on edge than ever, even though he didn't understand what was said.

"He and his men, they freed us, and at great cost to his own people," Kamal said, and showed Gorman a strange smile. "He has something for us that will help us defeat our enemies once and for all."

"You trust this man?"

"I owe him, Abdullah. I intend to give him what he wants. We will cooperate."

The older man smiled, seeming to accept what Kamal said. Abdullah clasped Kamal by the shoulders. "Come, we will eat and drink. This calls for a celebration. I have been in mortal fear, thinking I would never again see you."

Gorman took charge, weary to the point of murder at this spectacle. "Look, Aziz, let's hurry this up. You want to see that merchandise so we can get this show on the road? Let's do it. I can't leave my choppers out in the hills like that, either. I need to find them cover."

"I understand," Kamal replied in English, then looked at Abdullah and added, "We need weapons."

Gorman felt ice go down his spine. There it was. *They* needed weapons.

"Come," Abdullah said, leading Kamal down the street.

Gorman and his men followed Abdullah and Kamal to a house at the end of the street. Gorman nodded at Miller, who held back a dozen mercs at the door. Then Gorman and Reuter and the rest of his mercs piled into the large, Spartanly furnished room behind the Islamic rebels.

Halfway across the room, Kamal looked back at Gorman, his gaze narrowed. "You understand, of course, my men and I will need weapons. We are, how do you say in America, all for one and one for all now?"

Some of the Arabs chuckled, but Gorman and his men weren't laughing.

"That we are, Aziz," Gorman said, standing inside the doorway, the harsh sunlight making the ex-CIA man's skeletal death's-head more stark and ominous looking than ever. "'Till death do us part.' That's another piece of American brilliance, my friend."

Now Gorman chuckled, and it was Kamal's turn to look uncertain. The mood in the room thickened with tension before Kamal nodded and smiled at Gorman, as if the Iraqi understood something no one else did.

"Why are we all so tense?" Kamal asked. "This is business, Major. I am quite frank when I say I am prepared to extend you my hand and work out our deal. I owe you, after all. You freed me. I consider you my friend, my brother in blood."

"So untense me, 'my brother in blood,'" Gorman said. "Get the money, I'll give you the merch and we can all live happily ever after."

"It will be done."

"It better be done," Gorman said, putting an edge into his voice, drawing a look from Kamal before the man nodded at Abdullah.

As Abdullah threw back a large Persian rug and lifted the double wooden doors on the floor, Gorman walked forward and stared down into the hole. He figured there were enough AKs and RPGs in that hole to take on ten armies of Allah's finest.

As if reading Gorman's thought, Abdullah stated in English, "There are also twelve crates of fragmentation grenades. Plus one hundred and fifty pounds of dynamite and plastique. And enough extra clips for the AKs to keep them barking out death for days."

Kamal plucked an AK out of the hole, rammed home a clip and cocked the bolt. He looked at Gorman and again smiled with an expression that the big American thought would be more fitting on a reptile. He felt his adrenaline race and was prepared to start blasting away with his SPAS and M-16 if Kamal so much as began to lift that AK in a threatening manner.

"Now we can go check out your merchandise," Kamal said.

Gorman smiled, chuckled and slapped the Iraqi on the back. "You know, Aziz, I've never considered myself a people-loving-people kind of guy. Even still, I've got a compassionate nature and I'm starting to kind of like you. I think we're going to take this all the way."

Kamal was still smiling, but Gorman read something else in the Iraqi's eyes. Betrayal.

"WE ARE ONLY PLAYING a hunch, hoping for the best while fighting time," Yerzim said, guiding the Land Rover in a northeast direction down the desert tracks, an endless barren wasteland stretching out beyond the vehicle in all directions, the sun of high noon blazing like a furnace from a cloudless blue sky.

Seated beside the Mossad man, Bolan said, "But from everything we know, it's a strong hunch. For starters you told me that when Gorman escaped, he was flying in a due northeast direction. Second the arms deal most likely, if you believed Kaballah, went down in Syria. If it's missiles Gorman has, then they aren't easily moved without being detected. I suspect he stashed them. If he's going to sell what he has to the

Iraqis, then we have to believe he stashed it close to the Iraqi border.''

Bolan looked over his shoulder to check on the rest of the team. Weisskopf and Marlin were in the back, facing each other, both the woman and the Special Forces colonel keeping them updated on Kaballah's course. Weisskopf was poring over her maps of Jordan, Syria and Iraq. Marlin had a grim gaze fixed on the homing console and hadn't taken his eyes off the small blinking light since they had broken the Jordanian border a little more than an hour earlier.

A radio console beside Weisskopf kept their team in contact with Yoraam, who was now on aerial recon with his team of twelve commandos. If and when they found something, Yoraam would contact the ground force immediately, and they would coordinate a simultaneous ground-air attack. And Bolan knew they were ready for battle. Behind Weisskopf and Marlin the rest of the hardware was laid out. Everyone had an Uzi subgun, and there was a crate with plenty of spare 9 mm clips in the back. There was also three RPGs with a crate of 40 mm warheads, meant to blow enemy aircraft out of the sky or decimate large numbers quickly. Add one last crate that held two dozen MK-2 frag grenades, and the four of them, Bolan knew, were ready to tackle whatever enemy numbers showed.

When the time came for battle, each one of them would attach a half-dozen grenades to their webbing. But would they have enough time to catch up to their quarry? Bolan wondered. Mossad had given them twenty-four hours to hunt down Gorman, Kamal and the others who had escaped the Israeli prison compound on the Sinai, or the Israelis had vowed to pull all the stops, maybe even send their army marching across the borders of Syria and Iraq. That, Bolan recalled, had come straight from Yerzim, who had received his orders from the Mossad director himself.

And it had surely helped that Mossad had quickly convinced top Israeli government officials to sanction an all-out hunt for Gorman and Kamal. The fact that both their respective governments had managed to keep the original extradition of Kamal to the United States out of the world's headlines proved now to be a plus. But it wouldn't be long before the disaster on the Sinai became world knowledge. When that happened, there would be an international demand to spare nothing in the pursuit of Gorman and Kamal.

"Colonel," Bolan said, "is he moving again?"

"Just started. Same direction. Due northeast."

Weisskopf looked at the console, frowning. "I don't like it."

"Why's that?" Bolan asked.

"Kaballah stopped for a good twenty minutes. According to my map, the spot was an Arab village." Weisskopf turned somber. "Mossad believes that there are many such villages in Jordan, as there are in Lebanon and Syria. These villages provide safe haven for terrorists who cross our border, inflict their damage or plot future terrorist acts then escape back over the border.''

"Kaballah was clearly suspicious," Yerzim stated. "He has driven hard and fast since he crossed the border."

"Meaning, as we suspected, that he had a specific place to go," Bolan said.

"Or places," Weisskopf added.

Bolan fell silent, checking the rugged desert terrain. North, the wasteland was broken by jagged chains of hills. Bolan spotted stone dwellings, then movement of head-clothed and robed figures. Camels, goats and sheep milled around the dwellings, and two Arab men were pulling a bucket from an artesian well. It all looked harmless enough, but Bolan kept his guard up. Weisskopf confirmed that was the village where Kaballah had stopped.

"He's stopped again," Marlin announced.

Bolan turned and saw Weisskopf checking the homing console against her maps.

"He's maybe fifteen minutes ahead now, due north," she stated.

Bolan met the woman's suspicious gaze.

"He smells something," he said, then broke Weisskopf's gaze to survey the desert, looking for anything that would warn him they were being led into a trap.

No one spoke as Yerzim guided the Land Rover north, closing on a chain of low hills. The ground became broken, and Bolan jounced in his seat as the vehicle rolled over the uneven terrain. They began to head up the steep incline for the ridge when Marlin turned on the homing console's audio. The loud beep warned them they were almost right on top of Kaballah.

Bolan checked the ridge in both directions, his combat senses on full alert as he gripped the Uzi. When they topped the ridge, the Executioner found himself staring down at the crumbled ruins of an ancient temple.

"There," Yerzim said.

Bolan followed the Mossad man's intense gaze. In the distance, just beyond the rubble of long-since-toppled pillars, Bolan spotted Kaballah's Jeep. The driver's door was open, and the vehicle appeared abandoned. Something felt terribly wrong to Bolan. As he turned to check the ridge to the east, he saw the figure pop over the rise. And that figure was armed with an AK-47, the assault rifle suddenly blazing.

Bolan ducked a millisecond before the windshield was raked by lead and glass shards exploded past his face.

AFTER HIS MEN had cleared the mines and unhooked the trip wires attached to grenades, Gorman led his mercs, Kamal, Abdullah and the other Iraqis deep into the cave. Behind Gorman the Mi-6 was shut down, grounded in the mouth of the cave, its searchlight bathing the tracked carrier at the very deepest corner in this hole in the wadi in a brilliant wash of light.

Gorman held back, watching as Kamal and his Islamic brothers stared in awe at the five missiles in the carrier. Then Kamal stopped, checking the ground and the cave's jagged walls, his narrowed gaze dark with suspicion.

"Relax, there aren't any more mines," Gorman assured the Iraqi, then tapped his head. "I've got the world's greatest computer right here. I know how many and where they were laid. Hell, I'm the next best thing to Allah, Aziz. See all, hear all and know all."

"You are also very lucky," Kamal said.

"Luck is for guys with no balls. I'll have to explain Gorman's Law to you sometime, Aziz."

"Weren't you worried about someone, even an animal, wandering in here and setting off the mines?" Kamal asked. "An explosion would have sealed the cave, possibly even alerted a Syrian army patrol."

Gorman shrugged. "What's to worry? I didn't plan on being gone that long from my merchandise. Besides, maybe I've got friends in the Syrian army." Gorman paused, irritated by the lingering suspicion in Kamal's eyes. "Look, we're at the edge of the Syrian desert. Nothing and no one, except maybe some bedouin, come this way. Come on, Aziz, I had to protect my investment. It's all here. I've delivered on everything I've promised you."

The merc leader ran a hard stare over the faces of his troops. He looked to the mouth of the cave and saw four of his men, bright, faceless figures in the harsh sunlight, standing guard. He felt the tension, knew his men were ready just in case the Iraqis decided to be martyrs for the cause.

Abdullah cleared his throat, tugging the AK-47 a little higher on his shoulder. "Only five missiles," he said to Gorman, his voice flat but edged with contempt. "And they are worth twenty million dollars?"

"Let me tell you people something about these missiles," Gorman said. "These are SS-20s. They're specials, Abdullah, meaning they are nuclear tipped. Let me tell you what kind of firepower you've got here. Each missile has a yield—or explosive punch, to put it more simply—of one hundred and fifty kilotons. Now, one kiloton equals one thousand tons of TNT going off in your face. I think you can figure out for yourself the kind of damage just one of these babies can produce. They've got a range of 3417 miles. If a man knows how to operate these, he can hit Tel Aviv blindfolded.

"Think about it before you question just how much they might be worth to Saddam. So far, my men and me have been the ones to take all the risk, not to mention the fact I've lost a lot of good people. I feel I'm entitled to name my own price. If I want fifty million, that's what I'll ask. But I'll settle for twenty."

Abdullah didn't look impressed. "And you want us to go to Iraq and bring back twenty million dollars. Just like that. What makes you think Saddam does not already have SS-20s?"

Kamal lifted a restraining hand. "Please, Abdullah, let me handle this. This is my deal."

"This is *our* deal, Aziz," Gorman retorted.

"And speaking of Saddam," he said to Abdullah, "if he had this kind of firepower, he would have already dropped it on Israel during the Gulf War. Not even the Russians are crazy enough to hand him something like this. Next thing you know, Saddam gets a wild hair and he's wiping Moscow off the map."

Gorman had center stage, so he grabbed the moment, wanting to jerk their strings and let them all know just how smart and just how crazy he was. "Hey, the Russians have gone democratic. There's no more revolution for them, that is, if you believe the hype. They want peace and stability in this part of the world more than anybody. Your country, Aziz, is down but it isn't out. Hell, at twenty million, with all the oil money you've got, I'm giving you people a bargain. I can put you on the map with this suitcase from Allah. Forget car bombs, forget suicide attacks on a bunch of unsuspecting Marines. You want to give glory to Allah, this is the ticket."

"So what you are saying is that you are crazy enough to deal with Iraq," Kamal said, showing Gorman that strange smile again.

"You had damn well better believe it. I've already staked my life on this deal—that's how crazy I am. I've got nothing to lose and everything to gain."

Kamal pursed his lips and nodded. "Very well. We need to talk. Alone."

Gorman gave Miller and Reuter a curt nod, then led Kamal away from the missiles. With his two men right on their heels, the big American took Kamal outside and headed down the gorge. Suddenly Gorman felt the snake in his belly, which demanded violent release for all the pent-up rage and tension that had accumulated since freeing Kamal and his people. Worried, he scoured the ridges of the wadi, a half dozen of his men high above him, on both sides, watching the sky and the surrounding desert. But most importantly, they kept vigilance on the Iraqis.

Gorman looked Kamal dead in the eye. "Are we going to do this or not?"

Kamal smiled. "You are crazy. Crazy enough, I believe, to lead even your own men into suicide in order to get what you want. That, I can respect—a man who wants something bad enough and is willing to die for it. What I want to know is, are you crazy enough to trust me to go to Baghdad, in good faith, and return here with twenty million of Saddam's money?"

"I would be crazy, Aziz, to trust you out of my sight." There. He'd said it, letting the Iraqi know just where things stood. "What I do trust is that your heart is in the Islamic revolution. I trust that Saddam will want what I have. I trust that Saddam would be very pissed off if he didn't have the opportunity to buy what it is I risked my life to get.''

Kamal stiffened with anger. "I told you when we discussed getting the missiles from the Russians that I could get the money you wanted. Nothing has changed. However, it will take maybe three or four days for me to contact the necessary people. Whether I will speak to Saddam personally—I cannot guarantee that.''

"Time, my friend, is not money here. Time is up. As we speak, I am sure that there is a very large, well-armed and very pissed-off force of Americans and Israelis looking for us. You've got twenty-four hours. I'll wait in al-Shuraq for your return. Twenty-four hours. If I don't hear from you by then, I'm pulling out.''

"And where will you go? How will you transport the missiles safely, without being detected and blown out of the sky?''

Gorman chuckled. "I've come this far. That tells me somebody somewhere kind of likes me. You can call it luck, you can call it fate, but I get the feeling I've been blessed. Another thing. Don't bring a bunch of Saddam's lackeys back here to inspect my missiles or tell me they need more time to come up with the twenty. All I want is a suitcase full of cash. Then I'll hand you over your suitcase from Allah.''

"How will we move the missiles?''

"You let me worry about that. I can disassemble them in a moment's notice, both the missiles and the carrier." He paused, then added, "What you also might like to know is that only my men and myself know how to activate and launch those missiles."

"Is that some sort of threat?"

"No. It's fact. Meaning I'm going to have to teach you people everything you'll need to know in order to operate those SS-20s. Meaning I'll also be charging a small instructor's fee."

Kamal gave Gorman a long hard stare. "Well, since I only have twenty-four hours, I suppose I should be going."

"I suggest you take some of the vehicles back at the village. Take as many of your people you feel you need. I can't fly you. Sorry about that, but I can't risk much more air movement right now. We're close enough to the Iraqi border that I don't think you should have any problem getting back to me within twenty-four hours. I can have a two-way radio set up at the village. When you're on your way back, contact me and let me know something. Now, if you don't mind, I'd like a moment alone."

Kamal gave Gorman one last hard look, then turned and headed back for the cave. Miller and Reuter joined Gorman.

"I don't like it, Major," Miller said. "All of a sudden I get the feeling our boy has got another agenda."

"Well, we didn't break him out for him to have another agenda. The guy swears to me he can get me that twenty million, and I'm going all the way with him."

"That was before he got caught by the Israelis," Reuter said. "And that was before you blew away one of his people."

Gorman smiled ruthlessly at his men. "But we've still got the missiles. In fact, just in case Aziz decides to get squirrelly on me, I want to be able to haul those SS-20s out here in the blink of an eye. I want them pointed east, and I want two of them activated and ready to fly."

Miller looked uneasy. "You have any particular target in mind?"

The smile stayed frozen on Gorman's lips. "How about Baghdad?"

9

Crouched beneath the dashboard, his Uzi in hand, Bolan gave the team a quick check for wounded or worse. As wave after wave of slugs pounded the Land Rover and drilled the canvas canopy with holes, Bolan found Weisskopf and Marlin hugging the floor, covering their heads. Yerzim flinched beneath the wheel as the hurricane of glass razored through the interior. At first glance the three of them appeared unharmed.

"Anybody hit?" Bolan shouted over the din of autofire and the heavy thud of slugs against the bodywork.

"Just pull out and get us some cover!" Marlin said.

"I'm fine," Weisskopf stated.

"Hold on!" Yerzim roared.

As the hellstorm blew out the window beside him, Bolan felt the vehicle lurch forward and glimpsed Yerzim with gritted teeth and savage determination hurl the vehicle over the edge. The Mossad man kept his face angled low against the steering wheel as slugs

tattooed the hood in ricocheting lines that told Bolan
there were more than a few enemy guns out there.

The Executioner kept himself braced low against the
dash as Yerzim sent the vehicle in a bone-jarring run
down the hill toward the ruins. Moments later the autofire began to fade, but slugs still punched holes in
the canvas and whined off the bodywork.

"Here!" Weisskopf said, handing Marlin and Bolan
two grenades before attaching two of the frag bombs
to her webbing. "That should even the odds some!"

Yerzim directed the Land Rover into a long sliding
skid before the vehicle came to a jerky halt behind a
low stone wall. As bursts of sporadic autofire raked
the air, Bolan was out and taking cover. Crouching
behind the wall as Yerzim, Weisskopf and Marlin piled
out of the Land Rover, Bolan scoured the ridge. He
saw why the terrorists had been able to ambush them.
Deep natural grooves were cut into the hillside, some
of the gulleys snaking together to form shadowy
pockets. And all around him Bolan found enough
rubble and crumbled pillars to hide determined am-
bushers. From the ridge a lookout could have moni-
tored the desert and alerted the others. All Kaballah
and his cronies had to do was wait until they rolled up
the hill then cut loose.

With the suspicious lull in enemy fire, Bolan
searched the hills. This time he spotted five shadows
scurrying from one of the pockets and moving down
the hill. The enemy was bunched tight together. Per-

fect. Bolan plucked a grenade, pulled the pin and gave Yerzim, Weisskopf and Marlin a curt nod.

"Dead ahead, twelve o'clock. Give me some cover fire," Bolan ordered, releasing the spoon and gauging the distance to the target as roughly forty yards.

Together Weisskopf, Yerzim and Marlin began spraying the hills with sustained bursts from their Uzis. Brief return fire from AK-47s peppered the stone wall, but the combined and deadly accurate Uzi leadstorm found two terrorist targets and forced the rest of the enemy force to secure cover in the gulley. As Bolan heard the sharp cries of pain through the chattering Uzi barrage, he pitched the grenade.

Then, out of the corner of his eye, he spotted three more figures with AK-47s surging down the hill to the east. The Executioner cut loose with a burst in that direction a heartbeat before the grenade blew, taking out the new arrivals before their brothers were decimated by the ensuing blasts.

Bolan glanced at his teammates, gesturing for Weisskopf and Marlin to take the fight to the west as he saw three more terrorists with AK-47s slipping into the ruins from that direction. Since they were combat-blooded professionals, Bolan was sure the others knew the drill. They had to take the fight to the enemy or risk getting pinned down and hemmed in by an obvious pincers attack. Yerzim followed Bolan down the wall as Weisskopf and Marlin peeled off to the west.

The Executioner darted behind a pile of rubble as Yerzim's Uzi blazed. He checked the terrain around his enemy targets as slugs whined off stone around him. Ahead the ground rose in a broken layer of boulders and jagged edges of tabletop rock. If he could gain higher ground, Bolan could seize the advantage as the enemy advanced.

"Cover me," he told Yerzim, who nodded and rammed a fresh clip into his Uzi. He began to spray the gulley where the three enemy gunners were moving toward them.

Slinging the Uzi and unleathering the .44 Magnum Desert Eagle, Bolan broke cover. Behind him the warrior heard the merciless chatter of autofire as Weisskopf and Marlin engaged the enemy to the west. Swiftly, as a line of bullets tracked him, he vaulted for the lip of a broken table of rock. Enemy fire from the hillside briefly ceased as Yerzim's Uzi kept stuttering and pinned them in the gulley. Swinging his legs over the edge of the rock, Bolan came up from behind a boulder. He spotted the enemy, dead ahead and below.

Having gained the upper hand, Bolan triggered the .44 Desert Eagle. Three peals of thunder rolled over the gulley, and three terrorists had their chests ruined by large-caliber slugs. As the corpses toppled to the ground, Bolan scoured the gulley then the ridge. Nothing. Where was Kaballah? Bolan scoured the faces of the dead below him, finding none of the three Arabs was their pigeon.

Turning in the direction of the firefight to the west, the Executioner watched as Weisskopf and Marlin leapfrogged ahead, using the rubble and the pillars for cover. The enemy had secured their own cover behind a low stone wall near the crumbled archway of the temple. Marlin and Weisskopf took turns covering each other while one of them advanced.

Weisskopf lobbed a grenade toward one end of the wall. As the bomb blew, taking out one of the terrorists and kicking him over the wall, she hurled her second toward the far end. As the second blast produced a bone-chilling shriek of agony, Marlin was leading her toward the temple.

From the higher ground, Bolan gave the hillside and the ruins a hard search. Suddenly he spotted a familiar face in the distance. With an AK-47 poised to fire, Kaballah bounded over the wall by the Land Rover.

"Kaballah!" Yerzim shouted.

Whirling, the man triggered his AK-47. Yerzim dived to the ground as a line of slugs ricocheted off the pillar beside him.

"Let me handle him," Bolan said, then leaped off the ledge, hitting the ground with catlike grace as Kaballah, firing on the run, raced for his Jeep.

"We still need him alive," Yerzim told the Executioner, but Bolan was on the move, not giving the Mossad man a second look.

With wild sweeping bursts, Kaballah kept firing his AK-47. A blanket of slugs sparked off the rubble around Bolan. Not breaking stride, he angled away from the Jeep. Knowing Kaballah was going for the vehicle, the warrior was determined to cut the terrorist off. He gave the ruins a hard sweeping glance, formulating a plan to thwart the Iraqi's flight.

Kaballah fired one last burst before jumping into the Jeep. As the engine gunned to life, Bolan leathered the Desert Eagle, grabbed a grenade and pulled the pin. Trailing a cloud of dust, the Jeep raced ahead but was forced to cut a path directly in front of Bolan because of the maze of rubble.

The Executioner picked his spot, tossing the grenade several yards in front of and to the passenger's side of the careening vehicle. A heartbeat later the blast upended the Jeep and slammed it to the ground on the driver's side, then flipped it on its roof.

Desert Eagle in hand, Bolan sprinted to the vehicle and cautiously approached the driver's side. He heard a sharp groan, then saw Kaballah's battered face poking out of the window. He reached down and grabbed a handful of Kaballah's curly hair, hauling him out of the vehicle. The man cried out in pain and broke away, falling to the ground.

"I'm done playing with you," Bolan said, lifting the big pistol and aiming it at Kaballah's face. "You had your chance."

Kaballah spit out blood and dirt, then chuckled. "What, are you just going to kill me?"

The .44 Desert Eagle thundered in Bolan's hand.

"WE MIGHT HAVE a serious problem, Major," Reuter said, handing the field glasses to Gorman. "The kind of problem we don't need right now."

Gorman crouched beside his right-hand man. Looking through the field glasses, he gave the desert to the south a hard search. Hell, Gorman thought, it seemed all they had left were problems.

He and Reuter were alone atop the ridge that overlooked the Arab village. Black jagged hills ringed al-Shuraq east, west and north, providing some line of defense against any ground strike force. And there were enough deep depressions in the hills for Gorman to hide the Mi-6 and two of his three Mi-24s unless, of course, the hills were given a hard aerial recon. What bothered him was the open no-man's-land to the south. From there any armored ground force could easily advance on the village, make a frontal feint while another ground force moved in from the hills.

Gorman didn't have enough men left to hold off any pincers attack, and he damn sure wasn't going to count on Abdullah and his cronies to help defeat an all-out assault. Luckily his other Hind was back with the missiles with the force he'd posted to guard the SS-20 stash. Miller, he knew, wasn't far from a radio, waiting for the order to launch the two SS-20s in the direction of Baghdad. The threat of wiping Baghdad off the map would be used only as a last resort. Spent missiles meant a serious cut in cash.

Then Gorman saw it. It was a shadowy but bulky shape, cutting low through the distant, shimmering heat haze. A gunship, light brown camouflage, maybe a Bell or an Apache. Gorman couldn't tell, but knew the IDF used both types of attack choppers. Finally the gunship flew off to the west before vanishing altogether moments later. Not good. Yeah, Gorman thought, they had problems, all right. Someone was hunting for them.

He lowered the field glasses and stared down at the village. There was a lazy but tense feel down there. Villagers ambled around the village, trading goods, hawking wares. It was just another normal day. Gorman was already thinking ahead. He stared at the minaret on the domed mosque at the east edge of the village and smiled. He needed another trump card, and he believed he had one—al-Shuraq.

"Well, Major? Twenty-four hours is an eternity to stay put in this hellhole and wait for Kamal to come back. I've got a very bad feeling about all this."

"So do I. That's why we're going to go talk to Abdullah."

"What's the plan?"

"First we need to find if there's some way out of this place. I'm betting, with all the hardware they've got stashed, knowing they're not exactly upstanding citizens of Jordan, they've got some contingency plan in case someone unexpectedly pops in."

"A tunnel maybe."

"Maybe. But what I really want to know is just how much Abdullah cares about these people. Maybe he's got a woman or kids in the village. You know, a soft spot for the little people."

Gorman smiled coldly.

Reuter looked concerned. "We've got thirteen men, fourteen if you want to include Baumstein, and that guy looks ready to crack. About forty of them left with Kamal. Still leaves us outnumbered, at least four to one."

"Tell our people to be ready if I so much as give them a nod."

Reuter paused, then said, "Major, there's something I've been meaning to ask you."

Gorman peered at Reuter and didn't think he cared for the ex-Recces distrustful tone. "So ask me."

"You don't have our money, do you?"

"No. I've got maybe two hundred grand in a Swiss bank account. I spent all available funds arranging this entire deal. Paying people off. Buying the hardware. Buying a Hind, here and there, piecemeal. Throwing some advance money to you and the others."

Gorman stared hard and deep into Reuter's eyes. "Look, we both know what we're doing now was set up and in the planning months ago, Reuter. We both agreed to go all the way, go for broke. We're in the bottom of the ninth inning, down by three, two outs with the bases loaded. Two strikes and needing a grand salami. I need this deal. Without it, we are some truly fucked SOBs.''

"You'll blow Baghdad back into the Stone Age, won't you?''

"You had damn well better believe it. Then we'll fly right over the smoking glowing rubble and sell those SS-20s to the Iranians. Hey, what are you so worried about? As long as we've got the guns and we're breathing, we'll make it. We've been in worse jams than this. You with me, soldier?''

Reuter broke Gorman's piercing stare. "I'm with you, Major. I didn't come this far with you to leave with nothing.''

"Good. Then let's go find out how sentimental Abdullah is.''

BOLAN STOOD with grim determination on his face, waiting as the rolling thunder from the Desert Eagle faded over the ruins. Weisskopf, Marlin and Yerzim gathered around the Executioner and stared over his shoulder. Bolan got the expected result from the first .44 round as Kaballah began to scream in pain.

Bolan watched as the Iraqi squirmed on the ground, clutching the side of his head. Blood poured through Kaballah's fingers, and as he stared at his bloody hand, he cried, "You bastard. You shot part of my ear off!''

"The rest of it goes next. Then I'll work my way down to your arms, then your knees."

"I knew it. I knew you were following me," Kaballah growled. "Something is wrong. Something has happened, or you would not have let me go."

"Something has happened, pal," Bolan told the Iraqi. "For you it could mean sudden death if I don't get some answers. There was a jailbreak. Your buddy Kamal is free."

Kaballah looked stunned, then sputtered. "Gorman. I knew he would do it. Did I not tell you? He is the devil in human skin."

"And for you it could be the fires of hell if you don't start talking," Bolan said in an icy voice.

The Iraqi froze, staring at the .44's muzzle, just inches from his face, before slowly putting his trembling hand back over the side of his head, checking his wound. The blood pouring freely down the side of his face, Kaballah looked at his crimson-soaked hand. He laughed as if the joke was on Bolan and the others.

The man stopped laughing a second later when Bolan triggered the .44 Desert Eagle again. He screamed as the slug exploded rock beside him, spraying stone chips against his face.

Bolan thought about the massacre in Tel Aviv and he strongly suspected the Iraqi knew more about Kamal and the arms deal than he had let on. One way or another the Executioner would get the information so desperately needed if Gorman and Kamal were going to be found.

"What do you want with me?" Kaballah rasped.

"You had some destination in mind," Bolan said. "I'm betting with your life it's the same destination your buddy Kamal would have at this time. Where would he go?"

Kaballah looked at Bolan with defiance.

"You've got three seconds, then I'll send you on your way," Bolan warned. "For murderers like you, getting into Paradise is a real long shot."

The Iraqi seemed to think about something, then smiled. "I know exactly where Aziz would go. The same place where he and Gorman made the deal with the Russians. What I want to know is, what is in it for me if I tell you?"

"A stay of execution, Kaballah," Bolan replied. "I think I speak for the others when I say we're no longer making you any promises. Where?"

Kaballah ran a hate-filled stare over Bolan and the other. "Al-Shuraq. It's a village on the Syrian border. Close to Iraq."

Bolan looked at Weisskopf then Yerzim. "Is it on Mossad's list of suspected terrorist havens?"

Weisskopf nodded, grim. "We believe it is. If it's where he says it is, we're close. Less than a hundred miles."

"It is a home for maybe sixty of my brothers in the Islamic revolution," Kaballah said in a triumphant voice, then laughed. "If you're asking me to take you there..."

"We're not asking," Bolan said. "We're telling you."

"Of course you are. I have no problem with that. For you, my friends, I will gladly take you down your own road to hell."

Bolan told Yerzim, "Put him aboard. I'll find something to tie him up with."

As Bolan walked away from the group, he heard Yerzim say, "We need to contact Colonel Yoraam immediately. Mr. Belasko, do you have a plan?"

Bolan looked back. "Yeah. And I don't think it includes taking any prisoners."

Bolan moved swiftly toward the temple, Marlin right on his heels. He spotted that haunted look in the colonel's eyes again and knew the man was going back to some distant time in hell. The colonel grabbed a headcloth off a nearby corpse and tossed it to the Executioner.

"Why don't you clean that scum's blood off your hand," Marlin suggested.

Bolan nodded, locking stares with the colonel for another moment. He cleaned his hand as best he could while Marlin went and snatched a *kaffiyeh* off a second corpse.

"We'll tie him up with this," Marlin stated, walking up to Bolan and staring the warrior dead in the eye.

"You want to say something, Colonel?"

There was a long moment of tight silence before the haunted look in Marlin's eyes hardened with steely resolve.

"I don't know who you are," Marlin began. "I look into your eyes and I don't see any agent from the Justice Department."

Bolan cocked a wry grin. "Don't worry, Colonel. I'm not CIA, either."

"Then what are you?"

"Let's just call me a concerned citizen of the free world."

Marlin nodded. "Somehow I can buy that. For one thing you don't talk out of both sides of your mouth like some CIA goon. When you walk with somebody in battle, you go all the way, for him and yourself. I look into your eyes and I see a man who has seen and known and dealt out plenty of death. I get the feeling your road, whatever started it, is something similar to mine. But you've still got that look I used to see in the mirror a long, long time ago. A look that says you still believe in what's good and right in the world and that it's worth fighting and even dying for."

Marlin paused. "You said you knew about Gorman and me. I want to show you something." He reached into his pocket and pulled out what Bolan suspected was a photograph. The colonel stared at the picture, then handed it to Bolan. "She was my wife. That was our son."

Bolan found himself looking at a picture of a stunningly beautiful Asian woman. Long raven black hair, smooth almond skin, full lips and sculpted cheekbones made her a woman who would be admired and desired by any man anywhere.

"That's the only picture I have left of my wife and my son," Marlin stated. "It was taken in the living room of our villa in Saigon. Right before they found her and my boy murdered. I've carried that with me wherever I've gone for more than twenty years."

She was sitting in a wicker chair, holding a smiling AmerAsian boy in her lap. She was dressed in a white silk kimono with gold brocades. The woman's smile was radiant, reaching her eyes, and made her expression glow with warmth.

"She's beautiful, Colonel," Bolan said, handing the photo back.

"Yeah," he agreed, a trace of bitterness in his voice. "And my wife and son look very happy."

"Why did you show me that?"

"You have to ask?"

"Gorman."

"I showed you that picture just so you know where things stand with me. I don't want any sympathy, I don't want anybody cutting me any slack. I was semiretired when the top brass gave me the assignment to come over here and round up those bastards and take them back to the U.S. I smelled something. I had Langley holding hands with the Pentagon. I strongly suspect I was sent here as a scapegoat or a target. Or both.

Gorman came out of hiding, and the CIA wants him all of a sudden. The CIA goons who tagged along with me obviously had a contingency plan. That's why Crueller went tromping off on his own. That tells me they either suspected or hoped Gorman would pull off the breakout. Don't know what it means, and I'm not sure I care, unless they get in my way. What I'm saying is, I want Gorman. I want to be the one who puts a bullet in him.

I've got cancer. They gave me less than six months to live. I won't be going home, and I can't go to my grave knowing Gorman is still in the world. Do you understand?''

Bolan held Marlin's grim stare, then nodded. ''I understand, Colonel. More than you think I might. But how can any of us make you promises we might not be able to keep? If Gorman's in my line of fire when the time comes, I can't pledge myself to your vengeance. If you get him, well, then you get him. I sincerely wish you luck.''

''Fair enough.''

Bolan again looked deep into the colonel's eyes. The warrior found himself liking the man. Marlin, he thought, was the last of a dying breed, a dinosaur in a world gone mad, where greed, power and corruption seemed more important than honor, loyalty and human decency. Yeah, Bolan liked the man intensely.

For a fleeting moment he thought about his own genesis, Pittsfield, the horror his family had suffered at the hands of the Mafia. It seemed a hundred lifetimes ago. Bolan shook the past out of his head.

"Now I get the feeling you'd like to say something to me."

"Another time, another place, I just might, Colonel," Bolan said quietly.

"Mr. Belasko, Colonel Marlin, we've got a problem."

Bolan found Yerzim striding his way, disgust and agitation almost visible on the Mossad man's face.

"Our radio was shot to hell during the ambush," the Israeli stated.

Moments later Bolan was back at the Land Rover, tying the Iraqi's hands behind his back. Giving the vehicle's interior a quick check, he found that the radio and the homing console were in smoking ruins. They were on their own, at least for the moment. But it could have been worse. A wild bullet could have set off the grenades.

Bolan addressed his fellow hunters. "Nothing's changed. Our pigeon here is going to take us, as he put it, down the road to hell."

"Four against how many?" Yerzim asked. "Sixty? A hundred?"

"I have to believe Colonel Yoraam will look for us when he can't radio us," Bolan said.

"So, we hope he links up with us at al-Shuraq,"
Weisskopf said, concerned.

"I don't see any other way."

Weisskopf had steel in her voice as she said, "Mr.
Belasko, let me say for the record, and I think I speak
for the three of us, that we don't go home until either
Gorman and Kamal and the other are accounted for
or we are dead."

Suddenly Bolan heard the familiar whir of rotor
blades, then two black Huey gunships rose over the
ridge. The gunships hovered over the hill, kicking up
a wall of dust. Bolan watched, waited, his combat
senses still on alert. Finally the gunships broke through
the dust storm and lowered to the ruins. There was a
death's-head on the fuselage of both gunships, and as
the warbirds closed on their position, Bolan saw dark-
garbed figures with aviator shades standing beside M-
60 machine guns in the doorways.

"They aren't our people," Yerzim said.

When the gunships touched down in the ruins, Bolan and the other found themselves face-to-face with
Crueller.

An M-16 with an attached M-203 grenade launcher
slung across his shoulder, Crueller disembarked.
Scowling, he approached the group.

"You people are really starting to piss me off," the
CIA man growled. "I think it's time we had a serious
heart-to heart."

"I couldn't agree more," Bolan replied.

GORMAN WATCHED as Abdullah pushed back the Persian rug, then opened the doors to the arms cache.

Gorman's men, including Baumstein, and Abdullah's forty-strong force were gathered in the room. The merc leader got the distinct impression that the Arabs hated his guts, but they knew that they had made their own pact with the devil and they were stuck. Gorman always loved it when the other guy didn't have a choice.

He looked at Reuter, who was puffing on a stogie. At the first sign that Abdullah might turn on him, a nod was all it would take for Gorman's men to cut loose with their weapons. Gorman broke Reuter's grim gaze, watching Abdullah carefully.

"I am afraid there is no tunnel, as you asked," Abdullah said. "However, there is enough room down there to hide fifty, possibly sixty men. Do you care to look?"

"I'll take your word on that."

"There is another such hiding spot in the mosque," Abdullah informed Gorman.

"What about vehicles? I see a lot of pickups around town, but do you have anything you've stashed in the hills?"

"Yes. There are three vehicles in the hills to the north, just outside of the village. They are hidden in a wadi but are for an emergency escape only."

"What about gas for the vehicles?" Gorman asked. "Any reserve fuel?"

"We have maybe two hundred gallons of gasoline in the hiding place in the mosque. Why all the questions?"

"Because it just could happen that some very pissed-off and well-armed commandos might come looking for us. I need to know what I'm dealing with here in case it hits the fan. Bear with me, huh? You guys have family in this village? The reason I ask, is that I need to know if I can count on you people to go all the way in a fight and not have to worry about guys getting weepy eyed about loved ones on me."

Abdullah's gaze narrowed with suspicion. "Most of us are Iraqis. We came with Aziz after the Americans and the Israelis ruined our country in what you would call the Gulf War. We found many sympathetic Jordanian brothers in the revolution here. Of course they have family in al-Shuraq. Some of my men, when it became obvious we were going to need this village as a base of operations for the revolution, they brought their wives and children from Iraq. You do not have to worry about our courage."

Hell, it was perfect, Gorman thought, just what he needed to know. Concerned family men. A mosque with a couple hundred gallons of gas. Things were looking up all of a sudden.

"As for my family," Abdullah bitterly told Gorman, "they were killed when the Americans bombed

Baghdad in a treacherous and cowardly attack on innocents."

"Hey, we've all got our own heartache," Gorman said, thinking the guy might be stupid enough to take a swing at him as Abdullah tensed.

Then Gorman saw an Arab suddenly burst through the doorway.

"Abdullah," the man said, "there is a helicopter coming this way."

Alarmed, Abdullah looked at Gorman, who cursed. The merc leader saw his men tense with combat readiness, but he sensed some panic on the part of the Islamic terrorists.

"You and your men, you must get into the hole," Abdullah said.

Gorman hesitated. "You and your men put your guns down there first."

"There is no time to waste. They could be Israelis or Jordanians."

"Do it," Gorman said.

Abdullah snapped a nod at his men. As the Arabs tossed their weapons into the hole, Gorman said, "If they find us down there . . ."

"They will not!"

"Just the same, you make damn sure no one—not

one of your women, not a ten-year-old kid—points a finger this way. I will not hesitate to start killing people. You understand what I'm saying?"

"Perfectly."

10

Waiting as the CIA man looked over Kaballah with seeming contempt then scoured the carnage among the ruins, Bolan counted at least nine black-garbed commandos in each gunship. There could be more commandos in the bellies of the warbirds, he knew, and with the dust kicked up by rotors it was next to impossible to get an actual head count. But they were well-armed, determined-looking pros: grenades attached to webbing, commando daggers sheathed on lower legs, hip-holstered pistols, plenty of spare clips for their M-16s. With some very bad gut instinct in his belly, the Executioner couldn't help but wonder just what the CIA's real angle was in all this.

Crueller addressed the foursome. "Looks like you people managed a nice little victory here. Not too shabby. So notch some terrorist blood on your belts and pack it up. I've already told you this is CIA business. No more Mossad, no Israeli storm troopers and definitely no Justice guys."

"Looks to me like you expected Gorman to break Kamal free," Bolan said, nodding at the gunships.

"I think I know what you're trying to imply, Mr. Justice," Crueller growled. "First of all, no, I didn't expect him to free Kamal, as you put it. And I resent the fact you just implied I could be on Gorman's payroll."

"Did I?" Bolan said in a flat tone, controlling his mounting anger and suspicion.

"That Gorman could do it, yeah, that was always a distinct possibility," Crueller said. "Besides, this is a special CIA counterterrorist strike force behind me. They've been in place in Israel for nearly a month now. In fact, they helped with the capture of Kamal. I believe agents Yerzim and Weisskopf can vouch for that."

Yerzim frowned, looked at Bolan and gave the warrior a weary nod. "That much is true."

"Well, here's some more truth," Crueller rasped. "I just got my orders, straight from Langley. Gorman is going back to the States, alive."

"What?" Marlin asked, a dangerous rage building in his eyes.

Bolan couldn't believe what he'd just heard, either.

"Yeah, I know, I maybe lied to you about that, Colonel, with my terminate-with-extreme-prejudice rhetoric. Things have a way of changing."

"Makes me wonder what else you might be lying about," Marlin said.

Cruller put his hands on his hips. "I should have said, going back alive if at all possible, and I'm to make damn sure it is possible. You need to understand, Colonel, Gorman has been all over the globe for almost twenty years. The man has made countless invaluable contacts, from the KGB all the way to Communist terrorist groups in Southeast Asia. He has made major drug deals with both the cocaine cartels in South America and the opium warlords in the Golden Triangle. He has done intelligence, counter-intelligence and paramilitary work for Uncle Sam on just about every continent. He has worked for but unfortunately used the Company to make himself rich and to obviously now finance his own private mercenary army. There's no telling how many operations he might have compromised over the years. We need to know what he knows. In the interests of national, possibly even global security we need to know how much damage he has done.''

''Why is it the CIA is so determined not to work with either the IDF or Mossad?'' Weisskopf asked. ''Or even your own people right here?''

''Because there's nothing you can do any longer, that's why,'' Crueller said. ''Gorman's our problem.''

''You're wrong about that,'' Bolan stated. ''Gorman and Kamal are everyone's problem. We're supposed to be on the same side. If you're not helping us, then it would seem you're here to either hurt or hinder.''

''What are you telling me, Mr. Justice?''

"I'm telling you that if you want to play it your way, you want to be the Lone Ranger who goes home with the trophy, then the way I see it, first come, first served on Gorman and the others."

Crueller heaved a breath, shaking his head in disgust. Then he gritted his teeth, drew in a deep breath and said, "This isn't about glory, Mr. Justice. This isn't about careers, trophies or vengeance. Let me lay some more cold, hard facts on you people. For several weeks now we have known Gorman is sitting on five—count 'em, five—nuclear-tipped SS-20s. He doesn't give a damn if Kamal lives or dies. The only reason he broke the man out was so he could sell those SS-20s to Saddam, using Kamal as a middleman. We know for a fact Kamal and his Islamic revolution are financed by Saddam's plundered oil money and that Kamal is Saddam's fair-haired revolutionary martyr and all that Islamic extreme fundamentalist shit. For all we know, Saddam could be sitting on billions, but whatever he has, it would be plenty enough to buy what Gorman is selling.

"Can you imagine what a hero this murdering bastard Kamal would be in the eyes of that madman if he rolled into Baghdad with those SS-20s? Worse, can you imagine those missiles in the hands of a lunatic like Saddam? One SS-20 alone could vaporize Tel Aviv. I don't think I need to tell you what five would do if they landed on Israel."

Bolan felt an iceball lodge in his guts. That kind of firepower in the hands of a madman like Saddam could create the worst-case scenario in the Middle East. But perhaps even worse still, there was no telling what a desperate maniac like Gorman would do if his back was pressed to the wall. He might even launch one of those missiles himself. Bolan exchanged looks with Yerzim and Weisskopf, reading the grim concern on their faces.

"What's more and just as important, the Russians want their missiles back," Crueller said. "They're a little embarrassed, not to mention more than a little pissed off. They're holding the CIA personally responsible for the return of their missiles. I'm not going into a lot of details about the arrangement we worked out with the them. All I'm going to say is if the Russians don't get their missiles back and we can't show them Gorman has been brought in, well, they might just send in a team of Spetsnaz killers to comb the Syrian or Iraqi countryside. And you'd better believe they would start killing anything and everything that moves to get their missiles back. Forget the new Russian society of free enterprise. There's still a lot of old hard-liners who don't give a damn what the rest of the world thinks."

"So what you're saying is the Russians are giving you your chance to patch up any damage Gorman might have done to international relations," Bolan said, his voice cold but tinged with wryness.

"You got it."

There was a long moment of taut silence as Crueller stared at the four of them from behind his shades, looking as if he were trying to decide how to wrap up this encounter.

"I'm out of here," Crueller said. "But I'm going to tell you this. If you carry on with your crusade, even though you might have been sanctioned by the Israelis—well, you get in my line of fire, I can't be responsible for what happens."

Bolan knew it wouldn't advance their cause to argue or bother coming back at the guy with a parting shot. The CIA man had just made a veiled threat. So be it. It was both too strange and too suspicious that Crueller didn't want to work with them. What was the man's real agenda?

Crueller hopped back into his gunship. He stood in the doorway, watching as the helicopters lifted off.

Kaballah laughed.

"What the hell is so funny?" Yerzim rasped.

The Iraqi seemed to be enjoying himself immensely. "It would appear your road to hell is going to be paved with many demons. What has the world come to when you cannot even trust the CIA?"

Bolan pushed Kaballah toward the Land Rover. "Get in."

SITTING IN THE DARKNESS of the hole, his men huddled around him, Gorman kept a tight grip on his

M-16. With nothing to do but ride it out and hope for the best, the merc leader listened to the voices, barking and shouting at one another out in the street just beyond the safehouse. He recognized the voice of Abdullah, shrill and pleading. Then heard someone, most likely a soldier, addressing a man named Colonel Yoraam, Israeli.

"If they've found our choppers . . ." Reuter began.

"Just be ready," Gorman whispered. "If that door opens and you see any face other than Abdullah's open fire."

It sounded easy enough, but Gorman knew it wasn't. They were rats in a barrel. It was tight and hot, and he could smell the fear all around him. There they were, he thought, the world's toughest mercs, and they could all be killed in the next moment, gunned down in a dark hole in a remote corner of Jordan. And just when he was about to turn maybe the biggest black-market arms deal in history.

Funny how life worked. All the good things he'd done for his country, Gorman thought: crushing brutal regimes in Third World countries to give the poor and the downtrodden a shot at democracy and a better way of life; all the thugs and dictators and criminals he'd terminated at the orders of the Company; arming and training the poor in countries where their voices were unheard and their lives were seen as insignificant by brutal warlords or dictators.

Now he was a hunted animal, just because he had smartened up long ago and seen how useless, how senseless, it was to try to change things when most of the people he had tried to help really didn't want to change anything for the better. It was just one revolution replacing another revolution, out with one dirt bag, in with another. Just because he now figured it was his turn to make a buck, finish out his days in relative peace and quiet, that made him an international criminal? Hell, almost everything he'd done had either been known by or sanctioned by Langley, at least up until a few years ago. The ungrateful bastards.

Suddenly Gorman heard the rap of boot heels directly above them.

There was a heated conversation in what Gorman took to be Arabic, with Abdullah sounding both outraged and pleading.

An Israeli barked something, then the sound of boots faded but sounded in the far end of the safehouse. If the Israelis so much as found a scimitar hidden in a drawer, Gorman knew they'd tear the village apart. If they got to interrogating some of the villagers, putting on some pressure in the form of a little torture, then Gorman knew his deal would be finished. With the grim awareness that they might all very well die in that hole, Gorman felt the sweat run, ice-cold, down his back. Every man in that hole held his breath.

They were directly overhead again. There was the rap of boot heels, then the sound was muffled a moment later. They stood on the rug over the doors, Gorman knew. That grenade of explosive violence in his belly was ready to blow as the silence became nearly unbearable. Any second he expected the doors to open and all hell to break loose. This was it. He knew the Israeli colonel was looking at the rug. Or was he?

Finally the Israelis moved out.

Still Gorman didn't move a muscle for a full minute. He listened intently, finally heard the voices out in the street fade maybe five minutes later.

"They know we're here. Someone in the village must have talked. They must have spotted the choppers."

Baumstein.

"Keep your mouth shut," Gorman snarled quietly.

Another few minutes passed, then Gorman heard the rap of boot heels again and the sound of the rug being pulled back.

Gorman aimed his M-16 at the doors, the assault rifle set on full-auto.

The doors opened, light bursting into the hole. Squinting, the merc leader looked up and saw Abdullah grinning down at him, enjoying the moment.

"They have left," the Iraqi stated. "You can come out now."

Somehow Gorman killed the urge to wipe that grin off Abdullah's face with a quick burst of 5.56 mm lead. When the time came, though, he wouldn't forget this moment.

KAMAL SAT in the front seat of the Jeep as they drove toward the remote outpost. They were now maybe twenty miles into Iraqi territory. It had taken a good four hours, driving a half-dozen vehicles from al-Shuraq, crossing the rugged, trackless wasteland of northeastern Jordan while fearing an attack from anybody at any time. Outside his brothers in the Islamic revolution, Kamal knew that everyone was the enemy. Especially the devil, Gorman.

But Aziz Kamal had a plan.

Darkness now blanketed the outpost and the surrounding desert like a veil of death. It was ominously quiet. At first the outpost, which was little more than a large tin dwelling with several GAZ-66 transport trucks and maybe a dozen tents shrewed at the base of some hills, looked deserted.

Kamal saw the door to the tin structure open, light from kerosene lanterns spilling onto the ground. Twenty men of the Republican Guard, all of them armed with AK-47s, headed toward the oncoming vehicles. Kamal stuck his head out the window and identified himself.

The terrorist got out, his men gathering around him. The reception he received was warm but not nearly as wildly enthusiastic as the one he had gotten in al-Shuraq. He could understand why.

There was a sullen anger about these Republican Guards. They had been beaten badly by the infidels, watched their families and friends die by bombings or starve to death when the war was over. Iraq was in ruins. No money, no food, nothing but anger and hope. Yes, like these soldiers of the Republican Guard, Kamal knew the fighting men of Iraq were regrouping now, waiting for the day when they could strike again, but strike bigger and harder. Gorman had just what the revolution needed to put Iraq back into world power.

Kamal waited as Colonel Hamil Diab slowly walked up to him. The sight of their squalid camp and the mutilated face of Diab made Kamal sick with anger and hungry for vengeance. The colonel wore a black patch over his ruined left eye, lost during the Republican Guard's fighting retreat from Kuwait. An explosion had also burned the left side of his face, the skin a blotchy purple mass of scars and lumps.

Kamal embraced the man he considered a hero.

Diab stepped back, smiling. "Somehow, Aziz, I knew the Israeli dogs would not be able to hold you. You have been in my prayers since your capture. God answered my prayers."

The way the colonel looked at him, with admiration and respect, Kamal gained confidence. He was about to ask the colonel to risk his very life and the lives of his men.

"We need to have a serious talk, Colonel. There is something we must do together, something that will make us heroes in our country for all time. Or something that will make us martyrs for the revolution."

Diab's lone eye narrowed with the glow of intrigue as he stared at Kamal. "I know about the deal you struck with Gorman. I know what he has. Let me say now, Aziz, my brother, whatever it is you have in mind, I will gladly go along with it."

"Good. We can talk as we drive."

"The CIA is going to make a deal with that bastard," Colonel Marlin said. "Mark my words, you heard it here. Gorman will be dead, by my hand, before dawn."

Bolan looked at the Special Forces colonel and saw something in Marlin's eyes that warned him the man could prove a liability in their hunt. There was a burning gaze of pure rage and hate in the colonel's eyes, unlike anything Bolan had spotted up to that point.

No one challenged Marlin's right to vengeance. In fact, everyone in the Land Rover seemed to freeze for a long moment, stare at the colonel as if he were something alien, deadly and scary. Yerzim, taking his eyes off the desert tracks, looked into the rearview mirror. Bolan and Weisskopf, flanking the colonel, both gave Marlin a long look.

Hard silence followed for the next few miles as Yerzim kept guiding the Land Rover skillfully over the rugged terrain. Bolan raised the infrared binoculars and gave the desert to the north a hard surveillance. Nothing but broken plateau and some low chains of hills. It was an empty black graveyard out there, with the ancient ruins of the temples and crumbled forts of long-dead conquering armies dotting the landscape every few miles or so.

Agent Weisskopf cleared her throat. "Colonel, I'm not sure why you wish to kill Gorman so badly...."

"The man murdered my wife and son more than twenty years ago in Vietnam. And to this day I strongly suspect the CIA was involved in covering for that animal. That's why."

The two Israelis looked stunned for a moment.

"I see," Weisskopf said, catching Bolan's eye.

The Executioner nodded. "I believe him."

"Then, Colonel, you have our blessing," Weisskopf said. "But please, we need to work as a team from here on out. It could well be just the four of us when he hit al-Shuraq."

Marlin didn't say a word. In fact, he seemed to Bolan to retreat deeper into his world of vengeance and hate.

"There's something else I must say," Weisskopf told Bolan. "Baumstein, much like Crueller said about Gorman, must be taken alive. If at all possible. Baumstein is a traitor to Israel, there is no telling how much damage he has done to the security of our country."

"Yeah, you're telling me we've got another asshole out there who might have compromised sensitive operations," Marlin said.

"Exactly, Colonel."

"Those are our orders," Yerzim added.

"I have no problem with that," Bolan said.

"Colonel?" Weisskopf prodded.

"I don't give a damn about Baumstein," Marlin said, and Bolan could tell the colonel didn't.

Suddenly Bolan sensed Marlin, now that they were close to the enemy, didn't care about anything or anyone other than Gorman. The colonel was a man very close to the edge, wound so tight it looked to the Executioner that he could snap at any moment.

They rode in silence for another few miles before Weisskopf voiced what was on everyone's mind. "You realize that if we don't link up with Colonel Yoraam we will be completely on our own."

"At this point, we know that taking Gorman and Kamal will most certainly save more than just one innocent life. If it's just the four of us, then that's the way it has to be," Bolan declared.

Yerzim questioned Kaballah about their direction, and the Iraqi smiled, assuring them all they were on the right road to al-Shuraq. Then, without warning, a searchlight swept over the Land Rover. Bolan was out of his seat, checking the sky, squinting against the blinding glare. The loud whir of rotors descended over them in the next moment.

Yerzim hit the brakes. Then, with the searchlight pinning the vehicle, Bolan saw the Huey gunship touch down dead ahead. Uzi in hand, Bolan shoved Kaballah out the door, the rest of the team disembarking behind the warrior a heartbeat later.

Bolan watched as a figure hopped out of the gunship, standing for a long moment in the wash of light.

"At ease, people."

The Executioner held his fire as he recognized Colonel Yoraam.

GORMAN BOUNDED into the belly of the gunship, taking the radio headset from Hammersmith, who said, "It's him." In the soft glare of the overhead lights, Gorman's mercs gathered around him.

"You got the money?" Gorman said into the handset.

Kamal's voice crackled back, "Yes."

Gorman didn't like it. He thought he heard engine noise in the background but couldn't be sure. Something wasn't right.

"That was pretty damn quick, Aziz. Don't bullshit me. Have you got the money?"

"I told you I have it. But we need to talk."

"What's there to talk about? We stick to the original plan. You get back here, hand me the money and we go get the merchandise. Real simple."

"I would like to go directly to the site. We can make the exchange there."

"No deal, pal," Gorman barked. "Get your ass back here, hand me the money, then we'll go. And it better be American dollars. I don't have any use for dinars."

When Kamal didn't answer right away, Gorman knew the deal was off.

"All right," Kamal said. "I can be back there in maybe four hours."

"Make it three. I get the feeling you're not that far away. Over."

Breaking radio contact, Gorman ran his death's stare over the faces of his men.

"He's going to stick it to us." Gorman paused, then slammed the radio with his fist. "Looks like we're pulling out and heading for Iran, fellas."

Reuter spoke up. "We don't have enough fuel to get to Iran."

"I'll think of something."

"What if he really does have the money, Major?" Hammersmith asked.

"I seriously doubt that he does. In fact, I'm betting our lives he doesn't. I gave him twenty-four hours, knowing it would take him that long to at least get to Baghdad and pry the money out of Saddam's hands.

No way. I've done enough deals like this to know it's over. He's coming back here to try and take what we've worked so hard to get."

Baumstein cursed, his face etched in despair.

"Okay, people," Gorman said, smiling grimly. "Looks like we're going to have to get ready a little surprise welcome-home party for our Iraqi friends. Hammersmith, in a few minutes I want you to go round up Abdullah and his revolutionary brothers. Tell them I need to speak to them in front of their stash house."

As Hammersmith nodded, Gorman told his mercs, "By the time I'm through with Abdullah, he won't be bowing to the east, he'll be groveling toward the west."

11

Right away Bolan could tell Colonel Yoraam didn't like the latest news regarding al-Shuraq and the SS-20s. He rubbed his jaw and seemed to ponder the intelligence, looking uncertain to Bolan for a moment, as if he were deciding how to proceed. There was no question in Bolan's mind what had to be done.

As he stood in the rotor wash and the glare of the gunship's searchlight, Bolan counted twelve commandos gathered around the Israeli colonel, all of them in olive fatigues and toting Galil assault rifles.

Everyone looked grim, but Bolan could fully understand and appreciate their concern. When they hit al-Shuraq they would be greatly outnumbered, and Bolan sensed Yoraam didn't like the odds. But Yoraam was a fighter, and his eyes betrayed he was as enraged and burning with a desire for revenge as the rest of them. Even still, Bolan knew the colonel felt responsible for the lives of his men, and he'd lost too many good soldiers back in the desert to just go into al-Shuraq with guns blazing.

Yoraam laid a steely eye on Bolan. "You know anything about this CIA guy Crueller? Any chance we've got another Gorman on our hands?"

"I don't know a thing about the man," Bolan answered. "But I can tell you he could be a problem. What his real agenda is is anybody's guess. I'd watch my back when it comes to him."

"I don't have time to call in reinforcements. What do you suggest we do?"

The Executioner felt their stares fixed on him. He wasn't sure if Yoraam was testing him, or if the Israeli colonel, like Marlin had sensed he was in the presence of a warrior who had plenty of combat experience and was asking for a battle plan.

"Fly in low, then set down maybe a klick from the village," Bolan said. "Approach on foot. Lock and load. If we don't catch Gorman and the others now, we could miss our chance."

"I can't believe I could have missed them during our search," Yoraam said. "That is, if Gorman and Kamal are even there."

"They're there," Bolan stated. "If it's a terrorist haven, then they'll have plenty of places to hide. Don't take it so hard that you didn't find them."

"And they'll be well armed," Yoraam said.

"What's the layout of the village, Colonel?" Bolan asked.

Yoraam gave it to Bolan. From the air the colonel had counted roughly seventy homes and as many vehicles, more pickup trucks and Jeeps than any other type of vehicle, which had originally made him suspicious, but even more suspicious after he had been told by an Arab man during their sweep they were all merely poor bedouin. The village was set in a wadi, surrounded by hills except to the south, where there was open land.

Yoraam said they could advance on the village from the west hills without being spotted, unless, of course, there were sentries. If sentries happened to sound the alarm, Bolan said they could pour on fire support with the gunship.

"Finding those missiles has to take top priority," Yoraam declared.

"With what we know up to this point, my hunch is they're stashed close," Bolan stated. "Get to Gorman, and we'll get the missiles."

Yoraam nodded at Kaballah. "What about him?"

"As far as I'm concerned, he's just along for the ride. Do what you want with him."

"Let's get in the chopper," Yoraam said. "Bring that terrorist bastard. If any more of my men die, well, there's a possibility he might end up with a bullet in his head."

GORMAN PACED THE GUNSHIP like a caged tiger. He knew what had to be done, but that didn't mean he had to like it. The deal now with Kamal seemed like wasted time, but perhaps it wasn't, Gorman thought. He had to leave a strange message behind, let whoever might be involved in a future deal know he wasn't someone to stab in the back. Damn, there was no way out of this current crisis other than to clean up the mess with Kamal. They'd rely on the full letter of Gorman's Law, then move on. Finally, aware his men were watching him, Gorman stopped and looked at Reuter, who flicked his lighter and torched a stogie.

"I checked their explosives like you wanted," Reuter stated. "Just like Abdullah said. Dynamite sticks look to have twenty-, and thirty-second fuses. Found detonators and remote boxes for the plastique. Should be no problem with the plastique. I can have it ready in two minutes. The old bastard saw me checking what they had and gave me a look, but didn't say anything. Get the feeling, though, he knows something's wrong." Reuter paused. "You going to do it, Major?"

The twenty-million-dollar question.

"They way I see it, there may be no choice." Gorman ran a hard stare over the faces of his mercs. They were ready; Gorman spotted the resolve to get on with the plan.

Reuter, blowing a cloud of smoke, said, "Oh, well. Maybe we can get thirty million out of the Iranians."

Gorman walked to the radio in the cockpit. He was thinking, at that point, thirty million wasn't enough. If the Iranians didn't want to do business, well, he would still have three missiles.

MILLER LISTENED to the wind howling through the gorge, felt the chill of cold air as it lashed through the belly of the Hind. He was thinking how dark it was in the desert at night, how eerily quiet it could be when a man knew he might not live to see the next sunrise. Like the others, he wanted his payday, and he was determined to go all the way with Gorman. Whether or not he could launch those missiles...

The radio crackled with Gorman's voice. "Cobra's Nest to Lion's Den."

"Lion's Den here, Major," Miller said into the headset.

Gorman's voice filled the Hind like a voice from the bottom of a tomb. "Activate two missiles. Next time you hear from me, you fire away. You got that? Two missiles."

"That's affirmative, Major," Miller said, his stomach tightening, his heart skipping a beat.

Then there was dead silence as Gorman ended the radio communication. Something had gone wrong, terribly wrong, Miller knew, feeling the night close in on him with a crushing weight. He hoped his voice hadn't betrayed any disappointment or frustration to Gorman. The guy was insane, but so were the rest of them. Hell, they'd come this far. . . well, there was no turning back now.

The wind howled with sudden and ominous strength through the gorge outside. The former SAS commando had never felt more alone in all of his life.

Miller looked at the ex-CIA specialist, Cronin, who was standing in the doorway. "Man says be ready to nuke Baghdad when he calls back."

SURROUNDED BY HIS MEN, all of them armed to the teeth, Gorman walked, bold and defiant, into al-Shuraq.

He spotted Abdullah and his forty-strong force standing on the sidewalk of the main street. The Arabs were tightly packed together. Nice. And Hammersmith, who had gone ahead to tell the Arab leader and his Islamic brothers to meet him outside the safehouse, stood beside a Nissan pickup, the truck's headlights on, bathing the entire group clearly in Gorman's sight.

With the M-16 slung across a shoulder and the SPAS-12 canted against his chest, Gorman gave the street a narrow-eyed surveillance. All of the box-shaped dwellings were dark and silent, with the exception of three homes where doorways were open and light from kerosene lamps spilled out into the street. Shadowy figures stood in the doorways, watching, but they were unarmed. Abdullah and his men were all holding AK-47s. They looked tense and scared to the big American.

Gorman's mercs spread out but kept their weapons low by their sides.

"What is wrong?" Abdullah said.

"Everyone here?" Gorman asked.

"Yes. You wake us up in the middle of the night—"

"Shut up and pay attention."

Gorman approached Abdullah and stopped six feet short of him. Clenching his jaw, the merc leader gave his men a quick look. Baumstein, Gorman noted, again stood outside his group. The Mossad man looked nervous and agitated.

Gorman steeled himself. He had already rehearsed his dialogue with his men. They would know when to do it. What Baumstein would do was anybody's guess, but he had chosen to leave the Mossad man with his twin mini-Uzis, hoping the guy tried something. Yeah, there were plenty of messes to clean up before moving on to Iran.

"Oh, there's plenty wrong, my Arab friend," Gorman told Abdullah.

Hammersmith, cradling his M-16, moved slowly out of the headlights, became a shadow as he stepped into the middle of the street.

Abdullah licked his lips, looking around with all the fear of a cornered animal in his eyes.

"First order of business, don't ever laugh at a man who can crush the life out of you in the blink of an eye," Gorman growled, then let the silence hang for a moment, drilling a burning, hate-filled gaze into Abdullah. He saw the Arab stiffen with defiant anger, but knew he had the guy frozen with fear and confusion. Gorman's Law did work. "Second, but worst of all for you, your friend Aziz is coming back here to break it off in my ass."

Abdullah stared at Gorman with utter bewilderment. "What?"

"Aziz, the ungrateful bastard, is going to stick it to me," Gorman rasped. "Meaning the deal is off and the party is over."

The SPAS-12 came down in Gorman's hand.

Abdullah's eyes bulged in shock and terror. "What are you doing?"

Gorman's autoshotgun pealed its deadly flame, signaling the beginning of the massacre. With the SPAS-12 exploding its load into Abdullah's stomach at point-blank range, Gorman's mercs cut loose with a merciless barrage from their M-16s. During the next heartbeat, Gorman couldn't help but enjoy the sight of the bloody hole tunneled open in Abdullah's stomach, his back exploding in an even larger burst of gore. As if he'd just stepped on a land mine, Abdullah was viciously kicked into the front wall of the safehouse by the blast.

Then Gorman turned his murderous sights on the other Arabs, all of whom froze for a critical moment in utter horror, long enough for the thundering SPAS to disembowel or decapitate three more of the Islamic extremists while the relentlessly chattering M-16s swept the Arabs with blistering lead and decimated their numbers within moments.

Gorman didn't flinch as the Arabs were scythed apart, spinning, dancing jigs of death. The Iraqis who survived the initial burst of autofire did what Gorman expected. They ran. But Gorman unslung his M-16 and began to mow down fleeing men with steady bursts. Still, some of the Islamic extremists, even as 5.56 mm lead tore into them, tried to fire their AK-47s on the run or seek immediate and desperate cover behind the vehicles lining the sidewalk.

Gorman stepped back and triggered his M-203 grenade launcher. A moment later the hellbomb turned a pickup truck into a fireball. Then Gorman heard the familiar chug of three more M-203s as his men quickly joined the fiery burial of the surviving Arabs. With shredded bodies cartwheeling on the fiery crest of the first blast, three more vehicles erupted into flaming wreckage a heartbeat later. While torn bodies skidded across the street or thudded to the earth, Gorman and his mercs put any wounded out of their misery for good with long bursts from their M-16s.

For long moments Gorman raked a grim eye over the carnage, the crackling of flames filling his ears. Then he heard Abdullah groan. He couldn't believe it. The guy was still alive, struggling to sit up, holding in his guts.

Down the street panic had broken out among the villagers, the bedouin scattering in all directions.

"Round them up," Gorman barked at his men. "Put them all in the mosque. Kill anybody who gives you any crap."

Gorman walked up to Abdullah, who stared up at him with pure hate.

Reuter fired a fresh Havanna, joining Gorman as the other mercs ran down the villagers, firing bursts into the air.

Blood poured from Abdullah's mouth. "You... bastard... why...?"

Gorman liked that *Why?* He leveled the SPAS-12 at Abdullah's face.

As a bleating goat ran past him, Gorman smiled coldly at Abdullah. "I decided it would be too dangerous to hand those missiles over to a nut like Aziz."

The SPAS-12 roared.

BOLAN MOVED up the back face of the west hills with the Israelis and Marlin. Beyond the jagged teeth of the ridge above them, he heard the brief stutter of auto-fire and distant voices screaming. Then he heard men barking orders and cursing in clear English. Sound traveled great distances out on the empty wastes of the desert, Bolan knew, meaning they had to be just as cautious in their advance on al-Shuraq. That they hadn't been fired on by sentries told Bolan that either Gorman couldn't spare the men or the enemy was occupied with something else in the village.

But the enemy was definitely in al-Shuraq, and there was no telling what they would find when they topped the ridge.

Bolan looked behind and saw Colonel Marlin struggling to keep up, his breathing raspy and labored. The Special Forces colonel gave Bolan a look that said he wouldn't welcome an offer of help. Sick and dying, Marlin was keeping himself propelled on the energy of pure hate and rage.

A good fifteen minutes later, when he topped the ridge and crouched among the commandos, Bolan took in the scene below. Black-garbed mercs moved with a frenzy up and down the main street. They were planting something near the east end of the village. Explosives, Bolan suspected. Fire from twisted wreckage outlined the enemy movements. Bodies were strewn all over the main street, marking the massacre that had taken place, making the Executioner wonder what had happened here and why.

"It's Gorman, all right. It looks like they've taken the village hostage," Colonel Yoraam said, looking through infrared binoculars. "Why?"

"I don't know. Could be Gorman's deal with Kamal went sour," Bolan replied, watching as two men shoved a man into a mosque.

The village was laid out just as Yoraam had said. Bolan figured the best way to move in would be to split up, put a pincers attack on the enemy from the north and south ends of the village where the streets met and joined the main dirt stretch the enemy controlled. Bolan told Yoraam the plan of attack. The Israeli colonel agreed.

Just as they were about to move out, the two CIA gunships with their death's-head insignia flew in from the south, the gunships descending to the main street.

"What the hell's going on?" Yoraam growled.

Along with the others, Bolan watched intently.

GORMAN FLUNG HIMSELF into a doorway as the gunships descended. He squinted as rotor wash whipped up whirlwinds of dust and grit, watching as Reuter and the others quickly took cover behind the vehicles down the street. Reuter had an RPG-7 in hand.

A voice from one of the gunships boomed over a loudspeaker.

"Gorman, listen up, this is Special Operative Jack Crueller of the CIA."

"Never heard of you!"

"I'm prepared to offer you a deal. It's over, Gorman. Throw down your weapons. There's no way out. Do it my way, at least you'll live."

Gorman laughed. "In a ten-by-ten cell the rest of my life with guys picking my brains twenty-four hours a day. Kiss my ass!"

Gorman caught Reuter's eye and barked, "Get rid of these assholes!"

WHETHER IT WAS Crueller's gunship that was vaporized inside a roiling firecloud, Bolan didn't know, but he could only watch as the flaming hull crashed into a row of stone dwellings, a volcanic blast of flame sand debris blowing over the street. Instantly the other gunship veered away but came under fire. Muzzle-flashes lit up the street, the gunship's hull sparking with the furious onslaught of autofire.

"There's our cover," Bolan told Yoraam as the hellish din of autofire raked the air.

"Let's do it," the Israeli replied.

Bolan watched for another moment as the gunship streaked away from the village, then went into a tailspin. The aircraft vanished moments later into the blackness of the desert beyond al-Shuraq. Then Bolan heard the crash from the distance.

"Marlin's gone!"

Bolan locked grim stares with Yerzim. Searching the ridge, the warrior found no sign of Colonel Marlin.

Bolan led Yerzim and Weisskopf down the gulley that twisted down into the northwest edge of al-Shuraq. Uzi in hand, searching for targets, Bolan was near the foot of the hills when he lost sight of the shadow he knew was Marlin. He'd seen the Special Forces colonel only moments earlier move with swift purpose up a dark back alley that ran parallel with the main street. Marlin had crossed the edge, Bolan knew. The colonel was on his own.

Hitting a combat crouch, Bolan checked the streets as he neared the foot of the hills, giving Yerzim and Weisskopf a quick wave to stop.

He was at the last point on the hills from where he could give the entire village one last surveillance before moving in. South, less than a hundred yards away, he spotted four M-16-toting mercs guarding the entrance to the mosque. In the firelight that wavered over the main street, striking the mosque in an eerie glowing band, Bolan strongly suspected the bulky bundles he saw the enemy had tucked in their waistbands were dynamite. Then he caught a whiff of gasoline.

He suspected the whole village was rigged to blow. If that was true, then it warned Bolan that Gorman and his men were completely insane, hell-bent on dying in this village if they had to while taking out as many people as they could.

Bolan was prepared to move out when he saw the convoy of vehicles roll into the village from the east. A half-dozen pickups and Jeeps and two GAZ-66 transport trucks halted near the carnage that was strewed on the sidewalk. A force of roughly fifty men, some of them wearing *kaffiyehs* but all of them toting either AK-47s or RPGs, piled out of the vehicles.

A slight figure with an AK-47 strode away from one of the GAZ-66 transports. Bolan watched as the Arab inspected the slaughter all around him. Because of the intense firelight, the Executioner clearly made out the face of Aziz Kamal, and Yerzim confirmed that the man in the middle of the street was indeed the world's foremost terrorist. Even from a distance Bolan could tell Kamal was enraged. Whatever had gone wrong between Gorman and Kamal, Bolan knew it was all about to hit the fan.

The Executioner moved out, quickly hitting the northwest end of al-Shuraq, leading Yerzim and Weisskopf into the killing zone.

KAMAL SAW HIS MURDERED brothers on the sidewalk and was filled with instant blind fury.

"Gorman!" Kamal screamed.

A moment later the terrorist saw the former CIA man he had come to think of as the devil roll right out of the flames and the smoke.

"I understand some of your brothers have family here," Gorman said, moving past the flaming wreckage, flanked by six of his mercs.

Kamal saw the M-16 in Gorman's hand start to swing up. There was something else in the American's hand, something small enough to fit in his palm.

"Looks like you brought reinforcements, Aziz. Thought I told you not to bring back any of Saddam's flunkies."

Out of the corner of his eye, Kamal saw Colonel Diab stiffen with anger.

"Throw your weapons down, girls, I might renegotiate the deal," Gorman said. "Unless, of course, you do have my money. In that case, hand it over. We can walk away, and everyone lives happily ever after. If you don't, I've got that mosque filled with everyone I left living. My men are prepared to blow it and everyone inside straight to Paradise."

Kamal couldn't restrain himself any longer. Screaming in rage, he cut loose with his AK-47. Then Kamal saw something streak toward him from out of the firelight, heard it whoosh right past him.

Next thing he knew he was diving to the ground, covering his head, as the ear-shattering blast rocked the night. A heartbeat later the buildings on both sides of the street erupted in a mountain of fire, and the world turned black on Kamal as he was pounded by rubble.

THE STENCH OF GASOLINE grew stronger with each step they took. As Bolan led the advance on the enemy, a series of tremendous explosions split the night asunder, creating an umbrella of brilliant light that momentarily, and very dangerously, turned night into day.

The four mercs at the foot of the mosque's steps spotted Bolan and his team. A split second before the enemy opened fire, Bolan kicked into something. Glancing down, he found that the entire sidewalk was soaked with gas and saw that the dynamite bundles ahead of him were placed at staggered intervals intended to obliterate the entire west side of the street.

"Head for the other side!" Bolan shouted at Yerzim and Weisskopf, firing his Uzi on the run. He caught one of the mercs with a 3-round burst to the chest, but not before the man dropped a flaming Zippo lighter into the puddle of gas. A line of fire whooshed instantly to life, racing down the street in front of the west-side stone dwellings.

Bolan and his two companions poured it on with their Uzis as they angled for the houses on the other side of the street, veering away from the tracking lines of enemy fire. From the south end of the street, Bolan saw muzzle-flashes suddenly stabbing the Stygian gloom. Yoraam and his commandos had arrived, their combined autofire kicking another two mercs off their feet. The last hardman at the mosque lit the fuse on a dynamite bundle and hurled it at Yoraam and his commandos.

The Executioner hit the dark doorway of an empty house as the first bundle of gas-soaked dynamite blew. With rubble and flames shooting across the street, Bolan shoved Weisskopf inside the door, then piled into the home behind Yerzim. The deafening roar of ensuing dynamite blasts seemed to last for an eternity.

After the last bundle erupted, Bolan swung into the doorway. Through the smoke and dust, he caught sight of several figures rounding the corner and moving his way, their weapons barking and slugs pounding the sidewalk and doorjamb. Bolan ducked back, plucked a grenade off his webbing and pulled the pin. As he tossed the grenade down the walk, Bolan swung around the corner of the door, firing his Uzi. The enemy bolted off the sidewalk, vanishing from sight.

Not hearing any screams of pain as the shrapnel blast rang out, Bolan armed and let fly another grenade, knowing the enemy had retreated deep into the houses, escaping the kill radius of the grenade.

Bolan cracked a fresh clip into his Uzi, then broke cover. With Yerzim and Weisskopf on his heels, the Executioner sprinted down the sidewalk, hurling one then another grenade ahead just as the second grenade he had pitched erupted in a doorway. There was so much smoke and dust drifting around him, Bolan couldn't tell how Yoraam and his commandos were faring, but the relentless chatter of autofire kept sounding from the steps of the mosque.

As the grenades blew in the doorways, Bolan heard a shrill scream of agony. One, then two mercs popped out of a doorway, their M-16s stuttering. With slugs whining off the stone above his head, Bolan drilled the two mercs into the doorjambs with long bursts to their chests.

Combat senses on full alert, Bolan moved on, watching the doorways beside him. Suddenly he heard autofire and a sharp cry of pain from behind. Whirling, the Executioner saw Yerzim pitch to the street.

A man with a mini-Uzi had grabbed Weisskopf from behind and jammed the muzzle against her head.

Gut instinct told Bolan he had come face-to-face with the Mossad traitor. Weisskopf confirmed it in the next moment as she cursed the rouge agent.

"Drop the Uzi!" Baumstein snarled. "Do it, or I'll blow her brains out. I've got nothing to lose."

Bolan glanced down at Yerzim. Holding his hands over the bloody hole in his stomach, the Mossad man groaned. Suddenly faced with this new crisis, the autofire from raging battles in the village became distant sounds to Bolan.

"You shot him in the back, you coward!" Weisskopf grated.

"Shut up. I could have killed all three of you, but I need you to get out of here. You, drop the Uzi!"

Bolan hesitated, then let the subgun slip from his hand, giving Weisskopf a grim look he hoped she acted on. Both of them knew there was no way out, that a desperate traitor like Baumstein would say and do anything to save himself.

The Executioner pulled the .44 Desert Eagle as Weisskopf suddenly threw a hand up, knocking the mini-Uzi away from her head before she speared an elbow into Baumstein's stomach. As Baumstein belched air, the wind knocked out of him, Weisskopf ripped herself free from his grasp.

The slug from the big .44 drilled into Baumstein's shoulder, shearing off a piece of flesh. As the Israeli slammed to the ground, Weisskopf descended on him, kicking the mini-Uzi from his hand, then pulling the other mini-Uzi from its shoulder holster. There was pure loathing on the woman's face as she drew a bead on Baumstein, who froze in fear.

"You wanted him alive, Weisskopf," Bolan warned.

"The man's right, Baumstein. I think living will prove a fate worse than death for you. But if Agent Yerzim dies, I will surely see you hang in Israel. If you get up and go for a weapon, believe me, I will kill you."

Yerzim coughed blood. Weisskopf moved to him and knelt at his side. She checked his wounds, then looked at Bolan. "I'll stay with him."

Nodding, Bolan moved out. Autofire still raked the air from the south and the east ends of the village, but it was becoming more sporadic from the east.

Bolan saw the merc on the steps of the mosque was keeping Yoraam and his commandos pinned down. The warrior took care of that problem with a thundering round from the .44 Desert Eagle and punched the man backward several feet before depositing him on the ground.

As Bolan rounded the corner, he took in the fresh carnage. Fiery wreckage was strewed all over the street, and the billowing smoke made picking out targets nearly impossible.

But he counted five shadows, all of them running hard past the flaming ruins of the convoy to escape the hellzone.

"Gorman!"

Recognizing the voice, Bolan spotted Colonel Marlin in the distance, leaping over the rubble and charging straight at his most hated enemy. In the firelight

Bolan saw the mindless rage in Marlin's eyes. Something told the warrior Marlin was doomed and it was over in the next blink of an eye.

Marlin's Uzi flamed for a brief moment, but Gorman was more accurate, his M-16 stammering out a 3-round burst that kicked the colonel off his feet.

Bolan sprinted down the street, but Gorman and his hardmen were fleeing in a flat-out run. The enemy slipped out of the village, vanishing into the darkness and out of the Executioner's range. A moment later, closing on Marlin, Bolan found Yoraam and his commandos approaching on his flank.

"Call in the chopper!" Bolan shouted.

"Where's Gorman?"

"He's gone. My hunch is he's headed for his gunships. No time to waste, Colonel. I'm going after him to try and keep him from flying out of here."

Yoraam gave Bolan a steely look but nodded.

His senses choked with smoke, Bolan moved toward the flaming wreckage to check on Marlin, fearing the worst.

He gave the devastation a hard stare, looking for any sign of wounded. But there was nothing other than the sight and the utter silence of death. The explosives planted by Gorman had done their deadly work. Once again the merc leader had won a victory. With the explosives having been planted so close to the vehicles on both sides of the street, nothing could have survived those tremendous blasts.

In the next moment Bolan discovered he was wrong. He heard a groan and saw something stir among the wreckage.

As Bolan closed on the flaming hulls of the Iraqi convoy, Bolan found Aziz Kamal struggling to sit up. Kamal stared back at the Executioner with hate in his eyes. The Iraqi cursed, stood and swept an AK-47 toward Bolan in shaking hands.

The Executioner put one .44 Magnum round through Kamal's chest, launching the Iraqi back into the fiery wreckage. For a moment Bolan kept his grim stare fixed on the man. Even though the terrorist was crushed, the warrior couldn't help but wonder how many more Kamals were out there.

Bolan continued on and found Marlin stretched out in the rubble. The colonel was gut-shot and dying fast. Still there was enough angry life left in the soldier for him to grab Bolan by the arm.

"Is Gorman dead?"

"Hold on, Colonel. I'll get you on that chopper."

Despair clouded Marlin's eyes. "I didn't get him...."

Marlin's head lolled to one side as the death rattle escaped his lips. For a long moment Bolan knelt there. The colonel had been denied his justice, had felt the sting of one final slap in the face. Bolan felt great sorrow for this good man whose world had been shattered so long ago. Gently Bolan closed Marlin's eyelids.

The Executioner stood. Tugging the RPG-7 higher up on his shoulder, Bolan went hunting for Gorman.

SINCE LEAVING the village behind a good twenty minutes ago, Bolan had tracked the mercenaries hard and fast into the hills. In the distance, just beyond the rise above him, he heard the hard breathing of men on the run, heard the sound of rocks tumbling. He was close.

Minutes later, topping the rise, Bolan heard the whir of rotor blades. Below he spotted two gunships in the gorge. He lifted the RPG-7 and sighted on the familiar shape of the Hind. He could take out only one gunship, and he hoped Gorman would be inside.

Bolan triggered the warhead.

THE EXPLOSION ROCKED the gunship and nearly tossed Gorman out of the fuselage. Enraged, he moved into the doorway, the roar of the explosion filling his ears. His other Hind, engulfed in flames, was crashing into the wall of the gorge.

Wild-eyed, the ex-CIA agent looked up at the ridge, spotting the muzzle-flash a second before bullets began whining through the fuselage.

Everything had gone suddenly terribly wrong.

"Get us out of here!" Gorman shouted at Reuter, who was piloting the Mi-6.

Gorman flinched as more slugs ricocheted through the hull. He fought down the sinking feeling of defeat and steeled himself with rage and grim determination. If he wasn't going to get what he wanted, then Gorman determined to take out as many Iraqis as he could. Kamal had obviously all along intended to stick it to him. Well, Gorman's Law would prevail.

Gorman was moving for the radio to raise Miller and tell him to launch the missiles when the console suddenly sparked from the impact of a wild ricocheting bullet.

Gorman cursed, then flinched as more bullets ripped through the fuselage. Who the hell was firing on him?

BOLAN STOOD in the doorway of the Huey. In the distance he saw the dark shape of the Mi-6, flying hard and low to the north over the desert wasteland.

The Executioner looked at Yoraam, who informed him they were in Syrian territory but that the Mi-6 was out of range for his rockets.

Bolan was grateful to the Israeli colonel, who had gotten the chopper to evacuate himself and the others with surprising speed. In fact, Bolan had been picked up not more then a few minutes after the Mi-6 had lifted out of the gorge. If not for Yoraam's quick reaction, the enemy could well have gotten away.

He gave Weisskopf a long look. The woman was sitting beside Yerzim, who was hooked up to an IV. She gave Bolan a solemn look, then she turned her murderous stare on the source of her fury. Both Kaballah and Baumstein had their hands bound with rope and wouldn't meet Weisskopf's burning stare.

Bolan kept a hard eye on the fleeing Mi-6. To the east the warrior saw the first rays of dawn breaking over the Syrian desert. A line of jagged hills suddenly dotted the desert to the north. Moments later the Mi-6 hovered over those hills, then began to lower.

The pilot informed Yoraam that the Mi-6 was landing.

"Drop me off, Colonel," Bolan said. "I'll go in on foot."

Grim, Yoraam nodded.

As soon as Bolan hopped out of the belly of the Huey, Uzi in hand, he came under fire from roughly twelve of Gorman's mercs in the gorge.

But Bolan's death sights were set on the Mi-6. He watched as three figures rushed from the transport chopper and surged into the gorge, their M-16s blazing. As slugs whined off the stone around him, he ducked for cover.

The Huey lifted off. Bolan waited for air firepower and got it a moment later.

As the rocket pods on the Huey flamed and its miniguns blazed, the Executioner moved down the side of the hill. Picking targets below, he triggered his Uzi and took out two dark-garbed figures a heartbeat before the Mi-6 was blown out of the gorge in a thundering ball of fire.

In the flames of the wreckage, Bolan caught sight of Gorman. And Gorman, the warrior saw, was running for a tracked carrier, two missiles already elevated and pointed east.

Firing on the run, Bolan was halfway down the hill when the relentless enemy fire forced him to take cover in a gulley.

A moment later he saw Gorman's mercs get a lethal dose of the poison they had inflicted on the Sinai prison compound.

As the miniguns on the Huey flamed, mowing down the hardmen at the base of the hills, Bolan came up firing his Uzi.

The Executioner's tracking line of 9 mm slugs ripped into Gorman's legs. Screaming, the merc leader dived to the gorge.

Bolan figured he was less than fifty yards from Gorman, who rolled onto his side, firing his M-16. Slugs shrieking off the earth around him, Bolan vaulted over a boulder, angling ahead of Gorman to cut him off, fearing the man was making a last-ditch attempt to launch the missiles.

The Huey lowered into the gorge.

All around him Bolan saw the enemy ripped apart by merciless minigun fire.

As Gorman hurled himself at the carrier, Bolan fixed a long sustained burst. A bloody line of holes marched up Gorman's side, but the man somehow dragged himself to the carrier.

Bolan drew the .44 Desert Eagle.

The ex-CIA agent hauled himself to his feet, baring a bloodstained grin at his nemesis.

With minigun fire streaking through the gorge beside him, Bolan drew a bead on his adversary.

"Who the hell are you?" Gorman sputtered.

"Death," Bolan said, "and I've got a message for you from Colonel Marlin."

As Gorman clawed for his side arm, thunder pealed from the Executioner's big .44.

When all is lost there is always the future

JAMES AXLER

DEATH LANDS®

Crossways

In CROSSWAYS, Ryan Cawdor and his companions emerge from a gateway into the familiar, but ravaged world of the Rockies. But this is not a happy homecoming for Ryan and Krysty Wroth as the past becomes a trap, and old debts may have to be repaid.

Hope died in the Deathlands, but the will to live goes on.

Don't miss out on the action in these titles featuring
THE EXECUTIONER®, ABLE TEAM® and PHOENIX FORCE®!

SuperBolan

#61438	AMBUSH	$4.99 U.S.	☐
		$5.50 CAN.	☐
#61439	BLOOD STRIKE	$4.99 U.S.	☐
		$5.50 CAN.	☐
#61440	KILLPOINT	$4.99 U.S.	☐
		$5.50 CAN.	☐
#61441	VENDETTA	$4.99 U.S.	☐
		$5.50 CAN.	☐

Stony Man™

#61896	BLIND EAGLE	$4.99 U.S.	☐
		$5.50 CAN.	☐
#61897	WARHEAD	$4.99 U.S.	☐
		$5.50 CAN.	☐
#61898	DEADLY AGENT	$4.99 U.S.	☐
		$5.50 CAN.	☐
#61899	BLOOD DEBT	$4.99 U.S.	☐
		$5.50 CAN.	☐

(limited quantities available on certain titles)

TOTAL AMOUNT	$
POSTAGE & HANDLING	$
($1.00 for one book, 50¢ for each additional)	
APPLICABLE TAXES*	$_____
TOTAL PAYABLE	$_____
(check or money order—please do not send cash)	

To order, complete this form and send it, along with a check or money order for the total above, payable to Gold Eagle Books, to: **In the U.S.:** 3010 Walden Avenue, P.O. Box 9077, Buffalo, NY 14269-9077; **In Canada:** P.O. Box 636, Fort Erie, Ontario, L2A 5X3.

Name:_____

Address:_____ City:_____

State/Prov.:_____ Zip/Postal Code:_____

*New York residents remit applicable sales taxes.
Canadian residents remit applicable GST and provincial taxes.

GEBACK11A

Don't miss out on the action in these titles featuring
THE EXECUTIONER®, ABLE TEAM® and PHOENIX FORCE®!

The Arms Trilogy

The Executioner #61195	SELECT FIRE	$3.50 U.S. $3.99 CAN.	☐ ☐
The Executioner #61196	TRIBURST	$3.50 U.S. $3.99 CAN.	☐ ☐
The Executioner #61197	ARMED FORCE	$3.50 U.S. $3.99 CAN.	☐ ☐

The Executioner®

#61188	WAR PAINT	$3.50 U.S. $3.99 CAN.	☐ ☐
#61189	WELLFIRE	$3.50 U.S. $3.99 CAN.	☐ ☐
#61190	KILLING RANGE	$3.50 U.S. $3.99 CAN.	☐ ☐
#61191	EXTREME FORCE	$3.50 U.S. $3.99 CAN.	☐ ☐
#61193	HOSTILE ACTION	$3.50 U.S. $3.99 CAN.	☐ ☐
#61194	DEADLY CONTEST	$3.50 U.S. $3.99 CAN.	☐ ☐

(limited quantities available on certain titles)

TOTAL AMOUNT	$
POSTAGE & HANDLING	$
($1.00 for one book, 50¢ for each additional)	
APPLICABLE TAXES*	$_____
TOTAL PAYABLE	$_____
(check or money order—please do not send cash)	

To order, complete this form and send it, along with a check or money order for the total above, payable to Gold Eagle Books, to: **In the U.S.:** 3010 Walden Avenue, P.O. Box 9077, Buffalo, NY 14269-9077; **In Canada:** P.O. Box 636, Fort Erie, Ontario, L2A 5X3.

Name:_____

Address:_____ City:_____

State/Prov.:_____ Zip/Postal Code: _____

*New York residents remit applicable sales taxes.
Canadian residents remit applicable GST and provincial taxes.

GEBACK11